VIRTUAL CRIME.
REAL PUNISHMENT.

TOM CLANCY'S NET FORCE™

Don't miss any of these exciting adventures starring the
teens of the Net Force . . .

VIRTUAL VANDALS

The Net Force Explorers go head-to-head with a group of
teenage pranksters on-line—and find out firsthand that virtual bullets can kill you!

THE DEADLIEST GAME

The virtual Dominion of Sarxos is the most popular war-
game on the Net. But someone is taking the game *very*
seriously . . .

ONE IS THE LONELIEST NUMBER

The Net Force explorers have exiled Roddy—who sabo-
taged one program too many. But Roddy's created a new
"playroom" to blow them away . . .

D0980946

TOM CLANCY'S NET FORCE™

THE ULTIMATE ESCAPE

CREATED BY

Tom Clancy and **Steve Pieczenik**

BERKLEY JAM BOOKS, NEW YORK

TOM CLANCY'S NET FORCE: THE ULTIMATE ESCAPE

A Berkley Jam Book / published by arrangement with
Netco Partners

PRINTING HISTORY
Berkley Jam edition / June 1999

The Penguin Putnam Inc. World Wide Web site address is
http://www.penguinputnam.com

ISBN: 0-425-16939-1

BERKLEY JAM BOOKS®
Berkley Jam Books are published by The Berkley Publishing Group,
a division of Penguin Putnam Inc.,
375 Hudson Street, New York, New York 10014.
BERKLEY JAM and its logo are trademarks belonging to
Penguin Putnam Inc.

PRINTED IN THE UNITED STATES OF AMERICA

10 9 8 7 6 5 4 3

We'd like to thank the following people, without whom this book would have not been possible: Marc Cerasini, for help in rounding out the manuscript; Martin H. Greenberg, Larry Segriff, Denise Little, and John Helfers at Tekno Books; Mitchell Rubenstein and Laurie Silvers at BIG Entertainment; Tom Colgan of Penguin Putnam Inc.; Robert Youdelman, Esquire; and Tom Mallon, Esquire; and Robert Gottlieb of the William Morris Agency, agent and friend. We much appreciated the help.

TOM CLANCY'S
NET FORCE™

THE ULTIMATE ESCAPE

Prologue

Julio Cortez took a deep breath as the plane he was in approached the runway. The storm they'd been flying through for the last half hour continued to lash the plane with high winds and torrential rainfall. Julio could barely see through the window at his side, much less check to make sure that the landing process was going as planned. The wheels of the airplane struck the rain-slick runway with a violent thump. He could hear the engine's whine and the whir of the jet's flaps as they achieved maximum angle, feel the plane shudder as it slowed down. Julio let out the breath he'd held in a long sigh. They'd made it this far alive.

The airport's tarmac was rutted and in disrepair, making for a rough ride as the aircraft taxied toward the passenger terminal. Under normal circumstances, Julio would be glad to be safely on the ground after a flight like this. But these were hardly normal circumstances.

Julio scanned the faces of the other passengers. As before, they all avoided his gaze, suddenly too busy with their reading material, their carry-on bags, or the person in the seat next to them to make eye contact with him or nod a greeting.

The same was true of the CorteAir flight attendants. Throughout the difficult flight, they'd been courteous, efficient, thorough—but never warm or friendly with Julio or his family. Not like they were with the other passengers.

No one knows if it is safe to acknowledge our existence yet, he thought anxiously, wondering when that would change— or *if* it would change.

As his father and mother fussed over his little sister, Juanita, Julio peered through the window, trying to catch a first glimpse of his homeland, a place he barely remembered from his earliest childhood. But all he could see in the darkness were sheets of rain running down the Plexiglas, and the glow of the red flashing lights at the end of the runway in the distance.

The aircraft slowed as the engines powered down. With a bump and a shudder, the airplane swung to the left. Finally the terminal loomed ahead of them, still partially shrouded in the misty rain.

The aircraft completed its wide turn and moved toward the dimly lit main terminal.

Corteguay's Termina Internacional was not large or sophisticated enough to receive conventional aerospace planes, so Julio and his family had flown into the small South American island nation on an old low-atmospheric passenger jet aircraft, a Boeing 777 that had undoubtedly seen two decades of heavy use.

Well, Julio reflected, *the trip from Washington's Dulles Airport to Corteguay's Termina Internacional was one I really didn't want to make anyway. The longer it takes, the better I like it.*

That realization made him sad.

It isn't that far in distance, he thought, *but it's a world apart nonetheless. I might as well be on another planet.*

A very, very dangerous planet.

At any other time, Julio would have regarded riding in such a primitive, low-tech aircraft as an adventure itself—it was not unlike flying in the aviation simulators he loved so much.

But tonight, Julio felt he had adventure enough just returning to the land of his birth.

He gave up staring out the window and turned toward his family again. As his mother and father attempted to calm the fidgety Juanita, Julio studied them, trying to understand what would compel his parents to return to a nation that feared and hated everything they believed in.

His father, Julio noted proudly, had put his best and most courageous foot forward. He smiled at his family as the pilot spoke over the intercom, welcoming them to the Socialist Democratic Republic of Corteguay.

Well, why shouldn't he smile? Julio thought. *Tonight, he ends his former life as a political exile . . . and assumes his place as a presidential candidate in Corteguay's first free elections in almost twenty years.*

Tonight, my father has come home. . . .

And I guess it's my home too. Julio had to keep reminding himself of that. He would much rather be safe and secure in Washington, D.C., where he'd spent most of *my* life, and where all his friends lived.

With an act of will, Julio pushed those thoughts aside and concentrated on the here and now, just as his father had always taught him to do. Julio pushed away all thoughts of personal happiness and security as well.

That was something else his father had taught him, not through words, but by example.

As the aircraft slowed, Julio turned to his mother. She had her hands full taking care of Juanita, who was struggling against her seat belt and trying to pull down the tray table at the same time.

Julio almost laughed despite his feeling of apprehension.

It was amazing how much trouble someone so small and so young could cause. *I'm sure I was never that ill-mannered when I was a child*, Julio decided, his memory selective and blurred by time. *Juanita will be a handful when she's a teenager like me!*

Julio watched as his mother gently disciplined the five-year-old. Outwardly, she was calm, and her words to Juanita were soothing. But behind his mother's eyes, Julio could sense a dark shadow lurking. He recognized it immediately.

Fear.

His mother was afraid. For all of them.

Julio felt it too. And so did his father, though the patriarch of the Cortez family hid his fear better than anyone.

And if he can do it, then I can too, Julio decided.

His father's brave facade served to remind Julio that the man he knew—the Nobel Prize–winning economist, human rights activist, and university professor—was gone forever. In his place was a politician and aspiring public servant, destined, if the people of Corteguay desired it, to bear the weight of a nation on his shoulders.

To achieve that goal, Ramon Cortez had to hide his true feelings from everyone but those he loved and trusted.

And perhaps even from them.

It occurred to Julio that they had all been magically transformed in a single day. Only a few hours ago, they were a typical American family living typically American lives. Now, in the course of a short airplane trip, they had became political agitators and enemies of the current government of Corteguay. Political activism was a hazardous occupation in a nation famous for its secret police, military dictators, and political repression.

At that moment, Julio's grim thoughts were interrupted as the aircraft bumped to a halt. A steady electronic tone echoed throughout the compartment, informing the passengers that they were permitted to unfasten their seat belts and move about safely.

But as Julio scanned the aircraft, he saw that no one was moving. The other passengers were all watching them, waiting to see what would happen, and who would be waiting to meet Ramon Cortez and his family when the aircraft's doors swung open.

After a few tense moments, those doors finally *did* open.

Fortunately, no soldiers or policemen rushed in with stun guns raised and tasers ready. Instead, Julio saw an unfamiliar but not unfriendly face waiting nervously, presumably to greet them. They had been promised a security escort.

Their escort turned out to be a timid little man in an ill-fitting suit, who clutched his hat in nervously fluttering hands. He smiled when he saw Julio's father.

As his father rose to greet the man, Julio exchanged glances with his mother. Her face was pale, but resolved. Clearly, no matter what happened, she was determined to stick it out.

The flight attendants moved aside to allow Julio's father to pass. Instead of shaking hands, his father and the other man embraced, and then the little man spoke softly into Ramon Cortez's ear.

Julio saw a look of relief cross his father's face, and that feeling seemed to be echoed throughout the cabin, as the passengers rose as one and began to file out of the airplane.

Struggling against the flow of passengers, Julio watched his father lead the man back to their seats.

"This is Manuel Arias," Ramon Cortez said. "He has come to meet us. My brother Mateo is waiting in the terminal."

Tio Mateo! Julio thought joyfully. This was an unexpected surprise. Mateo had remained behind in Corteguay, and had suffered much under the current regime. It was courageous of him to come to the airport and meet his brother as he returned from exile.

Julio remembered his uncle from his childhood, so long ago. Back then, Mateo had been a colonel in Corteguay's army, battling against drug-runners, narco-terrorists, communist rebels, and black marketeers.

Suddenly, Julio felt a warm flood of relief wash over him too. *At least someone we can trust is here to protect us,* he thought. *Surely we're in good hands with Uncle Mateo to watch over us!*

Hurriedly, Julio gathered up his belongings, then helped his mother with Juanita while his father spoke in whispers to Manuel Arias. When the plane was nearly empty of passengers, he and his family moved toward the exit.

As they stepped out of the aircraft, a pretty flight attendant with dark eyes smiled at Julio and his little sister, and he saw pity and concern in her eyes.

Julio's fears returned.

As they walked through the tunnel that led from the plane to the terminal, Julio's father turned to his wife.

"Mateo is waiting for us in the main terminal," Ramon Cortez said. "He has brought some friends to escort us and—at my request—several members of the international press. . . ."

His father's voice trailed off meaningfully, and Julio saw his mother nod and smile brightly.

Julio smiled as well. He understood the importance of the upcoming carefully staged media event. Once the world was aware of his father's return to Corteguay, there was nothing the socialist regime could do to hurt them—not without the whole world knowing about it anyway.

Now I'm thinking like a politician, Julio realized with horror. *When all I ever wanted to be was a fighter pilot!*

The walk down the tunnel seemed interminable. But as they approached the gate, Julio's father took his wife's and daughter's hands. Then he turned and smiled at his son.

"We are home, my boy," he said. "And the press is waiting to speak with us. All of Corteguay will be listening."

Julio smiled back at his father. "I will not disappoint you, Papa," he said. "No matter how stupid the questions that they ask sound."

Ramon Cortez chuckled. "I never thought you would, Julio," he replied. "You never have before. . . ."

Then his father's voice trailed off, and the man looked away from his son.

"It is I who want to make *you* proud," he whispered so softly that only Julio heard him.

As the Cortez family stepped out into the main terminal, it felt as if a hundred flashbulbs exploded in Julio's face, and dozens of reporters surged forward in a wave, shouting questions in a half-dozen languages, and frightening little Juanita.

In the crush, Julio saw his father step forward and shake someone's hand. Then they embraced, and sporadic applause could be heard from the press corps.

Julio pushed past Manuel Arias and looked at the other man.

It was his Uncle Mateo. Julio would recognize him anywhere. His father's brother looked tall and proud and hardly changed from the way Julio remembered him, except perhaps for some gray hair and a certain guardedness that came, no doubt, from living dangerously in a totalitarian police state.

The cameras whirred continuously as Ramon Cortez embraced his brother for the first time in over a decade. Then the two men turned and faced the journalists together as Julio, his mother, and little Juanita lined up behind them.

As reporters spat rapid-fire questions at the two men, Julio scanned the assembled journalists. He noticed that, while many of the reporters had cameras, and a few had videocameras, none of the journalists was equipped with holo-cams, not even the reporters from the United States, Japan, and Europe.

Julio remembered then what he'd learned about his homeland in a briefing provided for his family by the State Department a few weeks before they left the United States.

According to intelligence sources, Corteguay's few media outlets were not equipped to handle Holo-Net broadcasts, nor were any Holo-Net cameras or virtual-reality equipment permitted within the island nation's borders. All such technology was prohibited, even to foreigners. It existed, where it existed at all in Corteguay, out of sight of public officials and cloaked by the strictest secrecy.

Corteguay's television was strictly twentieth-century flatscreen. In rural areas, people didn't even have flat-screen television. They relied on government-controlled radio stations to provide news and information.

In fact, Corteguay's infrastructure did not have high-tech computers, digital processors, or even video-phones. Such technology was deemed subversive. The free flow of information was not permitted in this ''socialist democratic'' paradise—lest the people learn how backward and poor they really were. The importation of any high-tech device was punishable by immediate confiscation, imprisonment, and even death. Enough people had died trying to bring Corteguay into the twenty-first century that the black market in computers and high-tech equipment was almost non-existent in the country. While no such ban could be completely effective, in Corteguay it was very nearly so.

Julio scanned the airport, but all he saw were flat-screen television monitors. There were no virtual hookups, no holo-arcades, and the pay phones he saw were all voice-only. According to the signs posted on them, they could only be used for making local calls. It was a vivid reminder that there were no Net links here in Corteguay. At least not for private citizens, though it had long been rumored that the government elite had their own access to the Net, and their own doctors to install the necessary neuro-implants for full virtual reality.

But such freedoms remained the purview of the elite, and were deemed too important—and too dangerous—to be wasted on the masses. As long as he was here, Julio could not join his friends in virtual gaming, simulations, or even V-classes. Though Julio had long since resigned himself to missing this year's "A Century of Military Aviation" seminar and competition, he still suffered pangs of disappointment when he thought about it.

After all, he'd practiced so long and hard in the Smithsonian's Flight Simulation Museum for the annual event, it was a shame to miss it. And Julio knew that he had a better than average chance to be this year's Ace of Aces. He'd been trying to win that honor for three years now. Last year's winner, Pavel Ivanovich, was now in training to join the Russian squadron assigned to guard Moscow. Julio had come in second, behind Pavel. He'd won the jacket he was wearing in that competition.

Many past Ace of Aces winners were fighter pilots now.

A dream come true . . . Julio sighed longingly. But it was a dream that was out of his reach here in Corteguay.

Suddenly, Julio realized that Uncle Mateo had ended the impromptu press conference. Following Mateo's lead, Julio's father guided his family to a remote escalator that took them to an exit on the ground floor. As they moved through this all-but-empty area in the terminal, Julio tried to get close enough to his uncle to speak with him. But Mateo was busy supervising a group of men who appeared out of nowhere with his family's luggage in tow.

Somehow, Uncle Mateo had found a way to get them past Corteguay's rigid customs inspection.

Finally, Julio got close enough to tap his uncle on the shoulder. The tall, gray-haired man turned and faced his nephew.

"Tio Mateo," Julio said. "It's so very good to see you again."

To Julio's surprise, his uncle seemed reluctant to meet his gaze.

"Good to see you too, Julio," he mumbled hastily. Then he immediately turned his attention back to his men.

Undaunted, Julio tried to engage his uncle in conversation

once more. But he felt a hand on his arm and turned. The little man called Manuel Arias met Julio's puzzled gaze.

"Your uncle is very busy arranging security," Arias said quietly with a kind smile. "Wait until we get out of the airport."

Julio nodded, and followed his family through the automatic doors. Outside, the humidity made the air heavy, even though a canopy kept them out of the rain. Since this was South America, Corteguay was just starting its winter season, what there was of it. Julio was glad of his jacket as he walked along. Julio saw his father wink at him.

"Not like ho . . . not much like Washington," his father said in English. Julio knew that his father had stopped himself before he referred to Washington, D.C., as "home." And at that moment, Julio realized that this return to Corteguay was a sacrifice for his father as much as it was for Julio and his mother.

Suddenly Julio understood that his father did not want to leave the United States either. Ramon Cortez had returned, not because he wanted to be president, but only because he felt he had a *duty* to return, and guide his homeland through the twenty-first century.

With that realization came a new understanding of his father, and Julio had never been prouder of him than he was at that moment.

"This way," Uncle Mateo said, pointing to a line of unmarked, windowless vans waiting for them in the sheltered area by the terminal's entrance. Julio watched his uncle rush ahead and open the rear double doors on the largest vehicle.

"Get inside quickly," Mateo said. "It is for your own safety."

Ramon touched his wife's face tenderly as she lifted Juanita in her arms. Julio moved forward too, but suddenly Manuel Arias clutched his arm again.

"Perhaps the children should ride with me," the little man suggested.

When he heard those words, Mateo abruptly froze in his tracks. Then he turned and faced the little man.

"Let us stick to the plan," Mateo said with a hint of annoyance. But Manuel Arias still clutched Julio's arm.

"The boy could ride with me," Manuel offered. "I could use the company. . . ."

Julio saw that his father had already helped his mother and sister into the van, and was climbing in after them. Mateo stared at Manuel Arias for a long moment, and some secret thing passed between the two men. Julio felt the pressure on his arm vanish.

Mateo approached his nephew. He smiled at Julio and touched his shoulder, pushing him toward the van.

"I think you should ride with the rest of your family," Uncle Mateo said. "It is for your own safety and security."

Julio suddenly felt a wave of suspicion flood his senses. He swung around and looked at Manuel Arias, but the little man would not meet his gaze.

Then Julio noticed that the other men who met them at the airport were lined up in military fashion, waiting for Julio to enter the vehicle. They were staring at him strangely.

"Wait, I—" But before Julio could finish, his uncle pushed him into the van so forcibly that he stumbled.

"Careful, Julio," his mother said, startled.

Julio looked up just in time to see his father's face turn pale as he gazed past his son. Julio turned and saw Mateo blocking the door, a look of cruel triumph on his face.

Behind his uncle, Manuel Arias stood, clutching his hat.

Then the van door slammed shut, and the lock clicked. The windowless interior was plunged into total darkness. Julio heard his father's body slam against the door, his fists pounding on the metal.

The van lurched forward and the tires squealed as the vehicle pulled rapidly away from the curb. Julio heard his mother's gasp of shock and fear and his little sister's cries of panic.

Poor Juanita is still afraid of the dark, Julio thought. Then, in the darkness, he heard his father whispering.

"I'm sorry, so sorry. . . ." he said.

A hissing sound followed, and a strange odor filled the van. Julio sniffed the air once. Then he knew no more. . . .

I

As the first streaks of dawn appeared over the horizon, a line of five Sopwith Camel biplanes bumped along a farmer's rutted field, engines humming. Their wooden propellers kicked up dirt and loose grass in the backwash. A fine mist of hot castor oil—used to lubricate the engines—accompanied the debris, spattering Matt Hunter's goggles and smelling to high heaven. Matt could see the canvas wings of his aircraft ripple as the air rushed over them.

As the planes neared the tree line at the far end of the dirt runway, four of the five Camels left the ground and climbed slowly into the brightening sky. Matt guided his craft into a slow circle around the field as he waited for the last plane to take off.

"Whoooooooo-eeeeeeee," Mark Gridley yelled as his Sopwith bounced off the field several times before it finally gained enough speed to struggle into the air and stay there.

Though his friend's biplane lumbered higher, Matt watched as Mark barely missed hitting the topmost branches of the tallest trees. Close call—Matt saw Mark take a deep breath and increase his speed to catch up with the rest of the squadron. Matt followed Mark until he was sure his friend was steady, then passed him to move into formation.

"About time you got here, Squirt!" goaded sixteen-year-

old Matt, his brown hair flying wildly as his best friend finally
slipped into place on his right wing.

Matt couldn't help but laugh with satisfaction as he remembered Mark's clumsy takeoff. It was a wonderful change of
pace to have finally beaten the whiz-kid at *something*. Though
only thirteen, the Squirt seemed to be a pure genius at all
things electronic.

Clearly that genius did not extend to handling century-old
aircraft technology.

Not that flying virtual reality, or veeyar, biplanes was all
that easy, Matt reminded himself. He himself had crashed and
burned on his very first flight—and his mother was a Navy
aviator, for pity's sake.

Not that she'd ever given him any pointers or anything. Her
career had left her little time for the let's-sit-down-to-dinner-
now kind of family life you saw on the holos. But Matt got
the definite impression she was betting on her aviation skills
being genetic. *He* certainly was.

Matt loved to fly any flight simulator he had access to in
the virtual world, and he was taking real-life hang glider les-
sons in his spare time. Matt was planning on becoming a real,
in-the-flesh pilot, as soon as the law and family finances allowed it.

Matt looked over at Mark Gridley's Sopwith Camel, just to
see how things were going. That was when Matt noticed that
his friend was making some of the same mistakes he'd made
when he first started out in this plane.

"Get your nose up, Squirt," Matt said, calling Mark, for
the second time, by his least favorite nickname. "And watch
out for that engine pull to the right, or you'll be leading with
your wing!"

"Roger, *Snoopy*," Mark replied tersely to his know-it-all
squadron leader. It was no wonder Mark was a little upset—
he was absolutely not used to being second best at *anything*.
But while he might be upset, he wasn't a fool.

Mark trimmed his aircraft just as Matt suggested.

"Hey, guys," David Gray said, waving at them from his
cockpit. "I think this 'Red Baron' stuff is going to be a lot
more fun now that we can actually *talk* about it while we're
doing it!"

Matt agreed.

Flying without being able to talk to one another—as they had up until today's simulation—had made Matt feel isolated and alone. And he was sure that the rest of the Net Force Explorers felt the same way.

It was more fun, and a lot less harrowing, now that they could actually communicate with each other.

"Oh, *yeah,* Dave ... this is *sooooo* much *fun,*" Andy Moore said with more than a trace of sarcasm.

"What's the matter, Andy?" David asked. "Afraid Baron von Dieter will shoot you down again?"

Mark, Matt, and Megan O'Malley all laughed. Even David Gray got a chuckle at his wingman's expense.

"Laugh if you will," Andy said with wounded pride. "But I've got a score to settle with the Bloody *Blue* Baron, and I'm going to even it *today.* Nobody shoots *me* down three times in a row and lives to brag about it!"

Everyone continued to laugh as Andy dipped his airplane's wings and waved his fist above his head.

"Remember," Andy said with more conviction than he felt. "Baron von Dieter is *mine!*"

The indestructible "Baron von Dieter" was, in reality, a fifteen-year-old German student named Dieter Rosengarten. Dieter flew a sky-blue Fokker Dr. 1 triplane with a battle face painted on the nose. He was the leader of the "Young Berliner" *Jasta,* or Squadron.

Matt and his friends were just beginning the first round of the internationally sponsored summer education course called "A Century of Military Aviation," which Matt Hunter had strong-armed five of his fellow members of the Net Force Explorers into taking with him. The course was set up both as an exploration of aviation and world history, and as a tournament, with teams from all over the United States and the world competing to take the trophy. Matt's team was running a person short because Julio had had to pull out after they'd registered, and substitutions weren't allowed.

In this first round, the Net Force Explorers had been matched up in a pool with several other groups to compete in multiple scenarios based on actual armed conflicts through the history of flight. Because the conflicts were based on real events, the probable results were skewed by things like available equipment, the relative strength of the opposition, and so on. In the interest of fairness, the results for each conflict were multiplied by a difficulty factor. The teams in a particular pool would meet each other several times in battle, and their aggregate scores would determine which team from that pool would advance to the next level.

There really weren't any losers in this competition, in Matt's opinion. Everybody learned a lot, got to fly the best simulators in the world, and had a good time. Though Matt wouldn't mind taking his team into the next round, where they would be working with simulators of experimental aircraft yet to be produced by the military and fighting in conflicts that had not occurred yet—and hopefully never would.

In addition to the team trophies given out, the best single pilot in the competition would win the Ace of Aces trophy. The prize, which was awarded to the most talented individual pilot in a given year, was a highly coveted one. Many former Ace of Aces winners went on to successful careers designing or flying high-tech fighter planes for their respective nations.

In this first week of the first round–competition, the Net Force team had been pitted against the German *Jasta* in World War I–style dogfights.

They'd usually lost too.

Dieter and his men had better, faster, and more maneuverable airplanes. They also seemed to enjoy their work. Even Matt, who had a little more experience than his friends, had been shot down by Dieter's Fokker on the very first day.

Though the mysterious Baron von Dieter had taken potshots at practically everyone, the German seemed to give Andy Moore *personal* attention. He'd shot the Net Force team's resident clown out of the sky the last three days in a row.

Needless to say, Andy was foaming at the mouth.

Part of the problem for Matt and his friends was the early twentieth-century technology they had to contend with in these aircraft. He and his friends, though they'd logged a lot of veeyar time as pilots, had spent most of their time in the simulators for current aircraft or those from the end of the twentieth century. They just weren't used to dealing with pre-computer-age engineering, and it showed in their "combat" performance.

Even Matt had fallen into that trap—he'd practiced almost exclusively in the modern simulators, because those had the most real-life relevance to him if he wanted to be a pilot. He'd assumed that flying was flying, that the skills learned in one plane would translate to another—something that was usually true in modern aircraft. It was now all too apparent that his assumption was wrong. He made a mental note to change his tactics when he started training for next year's competition.

Even though the Institute had computer handicapping—a programming feature that guaranteed that unless someone made a *really* stupid mistake, or was shot down in a simulated dogfight, their aircraft would remain aloft—flying the canvas-and-wood biplanes of yesteryear was still a daunting task.

"Flying the Sopwith Camel is like being strapped onto an engine with wings glued to your back," Mark had complained to Matt that very morning as they prepared for the simulated patrol. "I feel like I'm just holding on, like I don't really have much control over the aircraft."

Matt Hunter had to agree with his friend.

A few months ago, Matt had gone hang gliding in California with his dad. Though there was a very real risk of injury—or worse—when he was in the hang glider, Matt found virtual biplanes were much scarier to fly than *real* hang gliders. The biplanes were temperamental, full of quirks, and unreliable. But he'd discovered in the last week that he loved every minute he spent in them. They were a real challenge. He'd never have known what he was missing if he hadn't taken this summer class. He was glad he'd made his friends sign up for the course.

There was *another* reason—one much more to the point than unfamiliarity with the early planes, which was fairly common among the students participating—that the Net Force team kept losing to Dieter's Berliners. Right before the course began, the Net Force Explorers had lost their very best veeyar pilot.

Julio Cortez was the true Ace in their group, the only one of them who'd been in this competition before—in fact, he'd come within a point of winning last year's Ace of Aces trophy.

Though he'd been looking forward to trying for the title this year, Julio had had to drop out because his parents had moved. Julio's father was a prominent Latin American human rights activist and intellectual who'd decided to leave Washington, D.C., and return to his native land of Corteguay with his family. The country was about to have its first free election in twenty years, and Ramon Cortez intended to run for office.

Matt knew Julio's father was happy to finally be going home, but Matt was equally sure that Julio didn't want to return to Corteguay, a poor socialist island nation located off the coast of South America, a land with no freedom of assembly or expression. Corteguay also lacked access to the worldwide Net *and* to state-of-the-art hardware and software.

In almost any other country in the world, Julio could have joined them today. But not from Corteguay—and losing Julio was very bad luck for the Net Force Explorers. Julio had a knack for turning a disadvantage into an advantage. Take the Sopwith Camel's tendency to pull to the right. When Julio had flown this plane, he'd turned that into a combat asset, twisting and turning the plane in the sky like an old-time barnstormer.

Last year, when Matt and Mark had first met Julio at the Smithsonian's Flight Simulator Museum, there wasn't an airplane that the young political exile couldn't make his own. And in the last few months, Julio had only gotten better.

If Julio were here now, flying his orange tiger-striped Sopwith Camel, Matt doubted that Dieter's tally of six victories and no defeats would stand for long.

Matt wished Julio were here—both because he'd save their skins in the simulators and because Matt just plain missed him.

"Keep a sharp lookout," David Gray cautioned, his deep voice interrupting Matt's thoughts. "We're getting really near to the front, and close to where Dieter's *Jasta* jumped us last time. . . ."

Matt carefully scanned the sky above, squinting into the sun, but he saw nothing. Then he checked the low cloud cover for bandits using the cloud formations for camouflage.

Finally, Matt looked down at the ravaged landscape under his wings. The brown, blasted earth looked like a desert, with hundreds of parallel trenches and thousands of feet of barbed wire strewn across it. Occasionally, virtual explosions ripped up the ground beneath them as soldiers battled fiercely for every single inch of ground.

As the line of Sopwith Camels soared over the trenches, a terrible smell assailed Matt's nose.

"Phew!" Megan said. "What's that stink?"

Matt recognized the smell, but said nothing. He recalled experiencing a similar odor a few years ago.

After he and his dad visited his mother aboard the U.S. aircraft carrier *Ronald Reagan,* they'd gone on a side trip to Egypt. On their way to see the Great Pyramid, they'd ridden an open autobus past a newly constructed meatpacking plant on the banks of the Nile.

The stench from the slaughterhouse smelled exactly like the odor drifting up from the virtual battlefield below.

"Sometimes these programs can be a little *too* realistic," Matt muttered.

"Amen to that!" Megan agreed. Usually Megan O'Malley didn't like to show the least bit of squeamishness in front of the others. She was a tomboy through and through, and took pride in "keeping up with the boys." But the horrendous smell wafting up from the trenches would gag a Marine.

Everyone fell silent as they flew over the veeyar battlefield. If they learned nothing else from this virtual history course, Matt knew they would all remember the senseless, wasteful horror of war as it was practiced at the beginning of the last century.

When the group finally passed over the front lines and away from the smell, antiaircraft artillery was directed at their planes.

"Let's go a little higher," Matt said. Just as the words left his mouth, puffs of smoke and fire erupted in the skies all around them. The rest of the squadron followed his airplane into the clouds.

That was easy! Matt thought. *Yesterday I waved my hands until my arm almost fell off, but none of them noticed I was signaling.* The consequence of that bad communication had been the Berliners' *Jasta* kicking their collective butts.

Group communication was one of the few concessions made to modern technology in this veeyar educational program— but only on the last day of this level of the course, when the flying was supposed to be more of a competition than a history lesson.

All week, they'd flown just like *real* World War I pilots—without the ability to verbally communicate with each other.

It was difficult for Matt to understand how pilots could fight an enemy without adequate communications technology. Of course, World War I pilots didn't have adequate training, ejection seats, reliable planes, or parachutes either. Parachutes had in fact been available then, but the early fighter squadron leaders had resisted making them standard equipment.

The theory at the time had been that the pilots would fight harder if their lives depended on it. So the military on both sides of the war racked up horrendous casualty rates among their fliers, many of them preventable. All of the nations that fought the air war in the Great War lost more than half of their pilots to enemy action, equipment failures, and accidents. Most lost nearly eighty percent of their fliers. The Brits of that time referred to the Royal Flying Corps as "The Suicide Club."

No similar fate awaited the students in this seminar. Fortunately, another concession by the programmers was the placement of an *end program* or "Panic Button" on the dashboard of each aircraft.

If things got too intense, anyone could drop out at any moment by simply pressing the button.

Real First World War pilots didn't have *that* luxury. They went down with their planes.

As his team's "squadron leader," Matt Hunter also got an extra button, one that put a "bookmark" notation in the computer's vast memory banks, which stored the scenarios they were experiencing as they occurred. After the squadron had finished flying and was back at the Institute in real time, Matt could use his "bookmark" to call up the replay from the particular instant when he'd pushed the button. The function was perfect for settling disputes about who shot down whom.

As they flew on, deeper and deeper into "enemy" territory, Matt continued to scan the sky, searching for bandits, but the Germans weren't cooperating.

Just when it looked like their first flight of the day was going to be uneventful, everything hit the fan.

It was Megan O'Malley, from her position on the far left of the formation, who alerted the rest of them to the danger.

"We've got company," she said, pointing to the sky above them. "The Hun is diving out of the sun!"

Matt looked up, squinting against the veeyar sky's intense brightness. Then, through half-closed eyes, he saw them. Four dark silhouettes dropping down out of the sun's glare.

"Break off!" he said. As their orderly formation disintegrated, Matt veered his aircraft to the left, because he was sure that Mark Gridley would veer to the right.

Matt didn't want to lock wings with his own wingman. . . .

Before it seemed possible, Dieter Rosengarten's sky-blue Fokker triplane was among them, twin Spandau machine guns spewing virtual hot lead at the Net Force Explorers.

As the German flashed by, Matt pulled back on his stick, pointing the Camel's nose toward the sun. He was trying to regain some of the altitude he'd lost when the formation scattered, and get above his enemy. Matt knew that if he was flying too low, someone could easily chase him right into the ground.

Suddenly, Matt heard David Gray squawk. He turned just in time to see his friend's Camel lose its wings and drop out of the sky like a wounded bird.

"Bye now! And good luck . . ." David said as he hit the panic button. David Gray disappeared from the cockpit as the virtual Sopwith Camel plunged toward the earth nose-first.

Megan O'Malley was right there, coming in from above and behind the German plane that had destroyed David.

It too fell to the ground in pieces.

But Megan's revenge had its price.

Her plane was the next to fall.

As the rest of the *Jasta* attacked, she boldly turned her aircraft to face a lone Albatross fighter head on. The two pilots played "chicken" for a brief moment. But as they swerved to avoid each other, their biplanes locked wings in a violent mid-air collision that spun them around like a top.

This time it was the simulator's fail-safe system that dragged Megan and the German pilot back to reality, as the wreckage of their intertwined veeyar fighters plunged toward earth.

"That's *one* way to take out the enemy!" Matt shouted. But if anyone else heard him, they didn't respond.

Everyone still airborne was busy trying to *stay* there.

"Matt, I've got a problem," Mark Gridley said, trying to sound calm. Matt scanned the sky to locate his wingman. Finally, he spotted the Squirt, who was twisting his Camel through the sky in a futile attempt to shake off Dieter's triplane.

No matter what the young Thai-American did, the German pilot remained glued to his tail. Matt Hunter doubted he could reach his hapless wingman in time, but he knew he had to try.

Twisting his joystick and kicking his rudder control, Matt aimed his Sopwith Camel in the general direction of his friend. Just as he completed his turn, a German Albatross fighter dropped into his line of sight.

It was just too good a target to pass up.

Matt primed his single machine gun. Then he aimed and squeezed the trigger. He let go with a three-second burst, hoping that his only gun would not jam, as it had on the second day of the course.

To Matt's surprise, the Albatross lost its gull-shaped wing and burst into flames. A virtual bullet had shattered the control panel in front of the German pilot, and penetrated the fuel tank.

The German youth turned and saluted Matt. Then he quickly punched the "panic button" and vanished. His Albatross spun away in a cloud of smoke, fire, and debris.

Matt felt a surge of triumph. He had scored his first victory of the week.

Meanwhile, Mark Gridley had spotted Matt's Camel rushing to his aid, so he turned his own airplane toward Matt's. Dieter's triplane followed him, and when Mark completed his turn, the German was still doggedly snapping at his heels.

"Just keep out of his way for another second!" Matt said. "I'll get Dieter off your back."

The Squirt did not reply. He didn't have *time* to reply. Matt could see Mark was too busy maneuvering his airplane and dodging occasional bursts from Dieter's blazing machine guns to even think about talking.

Matt realized that there was a good chance that he was

going to overshoot his prey. He quickly snapped the Sopwith Camel to the right to bleed off some speed. But the violent maneuver was too much for the primitive plane to handle, and Matt lost control of his aircraft.

Matt fought the stick for a split second, barely preventing his aircraft from falling into a flat spin, from which he could never have recovered at this altitude.

But even as Matt regained control of his aircraft, he didn't have time to breathe a sigh of relief.

Mark Gridley's Sopwith Camel flashed by his left wing, and behind Mark, Dieter's blue triplane loomed in the crosshairs of Matt Hunter's gun sight. The German was coming at him head on. He was so close that Matt could see the "smiley face" that Dieter had "painted" on the nose of his virtual Fokker.

Instinctively, Matt squeezed the trigger.

His machine gun chattered—but only for a second. Then the machine gun jammed.

Matt groaned. *This is it,* he thought regretfully.

But just as Dieter's own guns began to spit virtual lead at him, a shadow fell across the unsuspecting German's fighter.

Like a predatory bird, a Sopwith Camel striped in a familiar orange-and-black pattern streaked out of the sun, gun blazing. The Fokker triplane veered hard to the left and fell into a steep dive as Dieter tried to dodge the torrent of virtual bullets.

But the German was too late to save himself.

As Matt watched, the canvas on the Fokker triplane's top wing was shredded by bullets and began to peel.

Both Matt and Mark cheered in triumph as Julio Cortez pounded Dieter's Fokker until the top wing broke loose and the triplane began to disintegrate.

Then, as suddenly as it began, the dogfight was over.

Hearts pumping with adrenaline, Matt and Mark guided their Camels alongside Julio's striped airplane.

"Julio, my man . . . you really pulled my butt from the fire!" Mark Gridley said joyfully.

"The Ace of Aces has arrived," Matt said, turning to peer at his friend. "It's really great to see you, *Jefe!*"

"Mark . . . Matt?" Julio said dazedly. "Am I here? Have I finally escaped?"

It was clear to Matt and Mark that something was wrong with their friend. He was acting like he was in shock, or had some kind of memory loss or something.

"Hey, Julio . . . what *is* it?" Matt asked. "What's wrong with you?"

"Nothing is wrong!" Julio said. "I've made it . . . I'm here! Matt, my good friend, I am here!"

"You're *here*, all right," Mark said. "And we're mighty glad to see you, *Jefe*. But what's the big deal?"

Matt struggled with the controls of his virtual aircraft as he stared at his friend. Julio's expression was one of confusion, as if he wasn't certain he should trust what he was seeing.

Suddenly, as Matt watched, Julio's eyes narrowed with determination. Julio looked directly at him.

"Matt!" Julio said urgently. "You must listen to me . . . my family . . . in Corteguay . . . you must do something, tell somebody!"

"Tell somebody *what*? What is it?" Matt asked. "What's wrong?"

"My family . . ." Julio said. "We are being held prisoners in my homeland . . . I have escaped for now, but I don't know how long I can remain free!"

"Julio!" Matt said. "I don't understand . . . are you saying that you are in a political prison . . . right *now*?"

"A *virtual* prison, my friend," Julio said. "Please . . . help me . . . help my father, my mother, and little Juanita!"

Then, as mysteriously as he'd arrived, Julio Cortez and his orange-and-black Sopwith Camel began to fade.

"Save my family!" Julio begged as he vanished, his voice hollow. "Help them, help us all, before it is too late. . . ."

A moment before Julio's airplane became completely transparent, Matt reached out and punched the buttons that would drop them back to reality and mark this instant in the computer's memory banks.

Abruptly, Matt Hunter and Mark Gridley found themselves back in their classroom, plugged into their computer-linked chairs.

The other three Net Force Explorers had already dropped out of veeyar or had been shot down. Now they were standing over Matt and Mark, staring at them with expressions of concern and confusion on their faces.

Matt and Mark exchanged puzzled glances too. Each of them wondered what they had just seen, and whether or not they should believe their senses—and what the virtual shadow of Julio Cortez had told them.

2

"I know it sounds weird," Matt Hunter said stubbornly, "but I'm telling you that we both saw Julio Cortez in that simulation. He was *there!*"

At his side, Mark Gridley nodded vigorously. Then the young Thai-American brushed his black bangs off his forehead and leaned forward in his briefing chair. "Ask Dieter," Mark said. "Someone shot the German ace down, and it sure wasn't *me!*"

David Gray looked pensive, a sheen of perspiration gleaming on his dark brown skin. Megan O'Malley listened intently, no emotion discernible on her pretty face.

Only Andy Moore said what he was thinking. And he said it bluntly as he stared at his two friends, shaking his head dubiously.

"I think you got bounced around so much in those biplanes that it scrambled your brains!" he said.

"All right, all right," Dr. Dale Lanier, the course instructor, said. "Everybody just calm down and we'll straighten all this out. . . ."

"Dr. Lanier," one of the technicians called from his control station. "We're ready to engage the holo-projectors."

"You just wait," Mark said to the rest of the Net Force Explores. "You'll see that we're telling you the truth."

As the lights dimmed, the Net Force Explorers faced the

briefing chairs on the opposite side of the [...]
had been looking forward to this moment, a[...]
excited.

After a week of competition, Net Force wa[...]
the pilots of the Berliner *Jasta* for the first ti[...]
simulator. Of course, Dieter Rosengarten and his [...]
still in Germany, but the holo-projectors in the b[...]
would make it look as if the Germans were right t[...]re, in the
same room, across from Net Force.

The same thing would happen in Germany, where holograms of the Net Force "Squadron" would appear in the same
room with the German team.

As everyone waited with anticipation, there was a burst of
light and color as the holographic projectors sprang to life.

Suddenly, a short, chubby blond youth with a ruddy com-
plexion, thick glasses, and a prominent overbite appeared. He
was standing in front of a group of smiling German youths
wearing identical black overalls.

Megan, who usually hid her feelings pretty well, actually
gasped in astonishment when she saw the formidable "Baron
von Dieter" for the first time outside of veeyar.

Dieter Rosengarten was much less impressive on the ground
than he was at the controls of a Fokker Dr. 1. His eyes looked
tiny behind his thick glasses, and it was obvious that his eye-
sight was so bad that corrective surgery was out of the question. The portly German youth squinted at them as he scanned
their faces.

On seeing the physically-less-than-formidable Dieter for the
first time, Matt was instantly reminded of the truth of his in-
ventor father's favorite expression.

*The real world and the virtual world are very different
places.*

To Mark Gridley, Dieter's appearance came as much less
of a revelation. As the shortest *and* youngest member of the
Net Force Explorers, "the Squirt" had learned early on that
in veeyar, you didn't need to be big, or strong, or fast.

You just had to be *smart*.

"Hello, everyone," Dieter greeted them jovially in English,
his German accent barely discernible.

"Greetings, Herr Rosengarten," Dr. Lanier said from be-

podium. "First of all, I want to offer our congratu-
ns to you and your *Jasta* for your success this week. The
erliner *Jasta*—and you, Herr Rosengarten—have reason to
be proud. You are the highest-scoring team at this point in the
first round, and Herr Rosengarten is the highest-scoring Ace
of the competition as it has played out so far."

Everyone applauded the Germans graciously, acknowledging their superior skills in the simulators, though there was a
less-than-gracious expression on Andy Moore's face as he
stared at Dieter Rosengarten.

If looks could kill . . . Matt Hunter thought.

The portly German smiled happily. "Thank you . . . thank
you all," he said with a curt bow. Then he turned to Professor
Lanier.

"I want to thank you, Dr. Lanier, for a wonderful week. I
found the class on the First World War very informative, and
look forward to the new phase of the course next week."

Then Dieter turned toward the Net Force Explorers.

"I also want to congratulate the young man or woman who
shot me down today." The German scanned the room through
his thick glasses. "Which one of you was it, please?"

"That's what we would like to ask *you*, Herr Rosengarten,"
Dr. Lanier said smoothly. "We were hoping that *you* saw who
it was. We're not quite sure which of the Net Force Explorers
deserves the credit." Professor Lanier paused. "There seems
to be some confusion in that regard," he concluded.

Dieter Rosengarten looked astonished. Then the youth
scrunched up his ruddy face in concentration.

"I assumed that the young man I was chasing looped over
my head as his wingman distracted me. An extremely nice
piece of flying." Dieter whistled softly in admiration. "Very
clever, I think," the German said. "And it was the first time
I saw that done in the simulator with a Sopwith Camel."

"I *knew* it was you, Squirt!" Andy Moore said.

"I *wish*!" Mark Gridley snorted.

Dr. Lanier gave Mark and Andy both a hard look, which
silenced them.

"You said that you *assumed* it was the plane you were
chasing," Professor Lanier said. "But what did you actually
see, Herr Rosengarten?"

"See?" Dieter said, blinking through his glasses. He raised his pudgy hand and scratched his double chin in concentration.

"Why . . . I saw my wing break off," he said after a pause.

The room exploded with laughter. Even Dr. Lanier smiled, something he did only on special occasions, like when describing the *blitzkrieg,* or talking about his own experiences in the air war against Iraq at the end of the last century.

During the laughter, Mark Gridley noticed that Andy Moore was staring at him with a strange new respect.

Andy still thinks that I shot Dieter down, Mark thought. *He's mad at me because he wanted to be the one to bag the German. But if I really did shoot down Dieter Rosengarten, why would I lie about it?*

When the laughter ceased, Dieter continued. "I'm sorry, Herr Doctor, but I never saw the airplane that shot me down. It all happened much too fast."

"Well," Dr. Lanier said. "I thank you for your help, Herr Rosengarten. And I thank you all for coming to this briefing. I want to wish you luck against Michael Clavell and the British team in the 'Battle of Britain' scenario next week."

"Thank you for the good wishes, Professor," Dieter said. "We Young Berliners look forward to altering the course of history and conquering England from the air."

The Germans waved a friendly good-bye to everyone and vanished.

"Let's just go back into the program, Professor Lanier," Matt Hunter said as the holo-projectors went off and the lights came back on. "I know what Mark and I saw, and I know that Julio is still in there."

"I think that's an excellent idea, though I don't think we need to go quite so far as to rerun the program," Lanier said. "Computer, bring up the summary grid for the Red Baron simulation."

"Working . . ." The synthesized female voice trailed off and the tally for the full World War I round so far appeared in the air above them.

"Excellent. Computer, bring up detailed information for participants Hunter, Gridley, and Rosengarten."

"Working . . ." Three small icons detached themselves

from the summary tally and grew quickly in size. Dr. Lanier studied them.

"That's odd," he said. "Dieter is listed as shot down at 11:38:26, but neither Mark or Matt are given credit for the kill. That shouldn't be possible. Computer, scan records for Contestant Rosengarten. Describe the terminal incident."

"Working . . . top wing disintegrated by machine gun fire. Resulting structural damage rendered the Fokker unflyable. Contestant Rosengarten pushed panic button and exited simulator at 11:38:26."

"Computer, which contestant," Lanier said, "inflicted the machine-gun damage?"

"Working . . ." The pause was much longer than usual. "That information is not available."

"What?" Lanier looked at the class in confusion. It was a look that sat oddly on the man's face, as though he rarely used his muscles to form that expression. "Computer, triangulate angle of machine-gun fire. Is it coming from a single source?"

"Working . . . plotting trajectory. Angle and velocity of machine-gun fire is consistent with a single aircraft-mounted machine gun."

"Computer, which contestant's aircraft was responsible for firing the bullets?" Lanier tried not to let his irritation with the situation creep into his voice, but it was futile. Thankfully, the computer was programmed to respond to his words, not his tone.

"Working . . . there is no plane in the triangulated source area of the bullets."

Lanier's face was a study in outrage.

"Sir," Matt said, "why don't we just replay the simulation? Surely we'll be able to tell what's going on."

At that moment a technician hurried into the room and handed Dr. Lanier a note. The instructor read it and frowned. "I'm afraid that won't be possible right now," he said. "The technicians just ran a systems check on the simulator."

"And?" Mark said.

"And we have a problem." The professor ran his hands through his short gray hair, and then held the note he'd just received aloft.

"It seems that our World War I program has developed a

Rift,'' the Professor said. ''We're restricting access to the World War I program disks, effective immediately. I'm afraid that no students can access them until further notice, not until we've brought in an expert to isolate and repair the problem.''

''I can't believe they're going to stop us from replaying the program because of a stupid glitch!'' Matt said bitterly to his friends.

The Net Force Explorers were resting in one of the International Educational Institute's many lounges.

''How can reliving what we've already been through once hurt us anyway?'' Matt wondered aloud as he scanned the faces of his friends.

David Gray met Matt's stare and shook his head. ''It isn't like that, and you know it,'' he said with a passion that surprised Matt. ''There's no guarantee that the program will stay the way you froze it, not if what I've heard about Rifts is true.''

''David's right,'' said Megan. ''Rifts are dangerous. You're lucky that nothing bad happened to you the first time.''

Matt was sure she was wrong. He knew very little about Rifts—and had, in fact, thought they were just another one of those legends. A Rift was a software glitch that supposedly broke down the boundaries between the computer and the user's mind. The user's thoughts, experiences, and feelings could feed into the program, and vice versa. Tales were told about kids who played games in veeyar, and came out of them with all of the injuries they had incurred while on-line. The whole thing sounded absurd to Matt. But before he could argue with Megan, he heard another voice.

''Well, I don't think it *was* a Rift,'' Mark Gridley said. ''I've heard about Rifts, and there was no sign of a Rift in that program.''

''You've *heard* of Rifts,'' Megan O'Malley said. ''But have you ever *seen* a Rift? Has anyone here seen a Rift?''

No one spoke for a moment. Megan focused on Matt, which made him squirm. He had no certain answer, because he just didn't know enough about Rifts.

''I've seen one,'' Andy Moore said finally, saving Matt from further embarrassment. All eyes turned toward Andy.

"A long time ago, I thought Rifts were just myths to scare kids away from adult sims and hazardous programs," he told them. "I got interested in them because I heard about Signal 30."

"You believed that!" David chuckled. Matt smiled in recognition. Megan looked puzzled.

"What's Signal 30?" she asked.

"There's an emergency rescue crew training veeyar called Signal 30," Andy told her.

"I heard it was an anti-drunk-driving veeyar," Matt Hunter said, recalling the urban legend from his own childhood.

"Whatever," Andy said. "Anyway, the story's about some kid who accessed the veeyar program when he wasn't supposed to. He got into a virtual car wreck where his head got cut off—"

Mark Gridley jumped in. "So they find this kid in his veeyar chair the next day—"

"And his head's missing," Megan said. "Which makes your stupid story predictable and absurd at the same time." She rolled her eyes.

"Quite an accomplishment, Moore."

"But *scary*," Matt added. "When you're six or seven years old anyway." He recalled his own reaction to the legend, which he heard years before. It had made him afraid of veeyar technology for at least a year.

"So what's this have to do with Rifts?" Megan asked Andy.

"When I was younger, I got into trouble sometimes," Andy confessed.

There were gusts of suppressed laughter throughout the room. David looked up. "Oh, *really*? I never would have guessed."

"Yeah, well, I used to mess around with programs to see if I could cause long-term effects, effects that would stay with a person after they'd left veeyar for the real world." Andy's voice got lower, until it was almost a whisper. "Once, I even tried to *create* a Rift. I didn't get far, and what I did manage to make wasn't all that interesting—just a lot of random activity, memory bursts, boring stuff like that."

"That's *so* admirable of you," Megan said, appalled. "You actually tried to make Mindcandy."

"I did not try to make Mindcandy!" Andy objected. "There was no such thing as Mindcandy back then. I was just, you know, playing around."

"Don't play like that again," David Gray said somberly. "Ever."

Matt stared at David, surprised by the threat implied by David's tone of voice. He knew that David Gray hated everything about the newest illegal kick available on the street—the cyber "drug" called Mindcandy. It was a very addictive and very illegal veeyar program add-on that directly stimulated the pleasure centers of the brain while playing a scenario chosen by the user. Matt knew that playing with the human mind was really dangerous, and that there were laws against such activity.

Matt also knew that David felt strongly enough about the subject that he thought anyone who messed with that kind of stuff should not be in the Net Force Explorers. Though Andy had always been a show-off, neither Matt nor David ever imagined that he would play with *that* kind of fire. They both decided independently that they'd better keep a close watch on Mr. Andy Moore. And Matt thought it might not be a bad idea to keep an eye on David as well, until he calmed down.

"Anyway, Signal 30 is just a folk tale," Matt Hunter said, getting back on the subject again. "It's a modern campfire story, an urban legend, nothing more."

"But you heard what Dr. Lanier said," Megan pointed out. "No two Rifts are alike. You can see—or imagine you saw—just about anything!"

Mark Gridley snorted. "The problem with that theory is that Matt didn't see it alone . . . *I* saw it *too*!"

"The real problem is that I didn't get to go after Dieter," Andy said. "If you had just let me handle the Blue Baron, we wouldn't be talking about this now, *Squirt*!"

Matt sighed. Andy knew that the hated nickname would get a rise out of Mark, and it worked. As Matt watched, Mark got livid and started calling Andy names, and Moore, older but no more mature than the Squirt, shot back a few childish insults of his own.

Things were degenerating quickly, and Megan turned, her eyes meeting Matt's in a plea for leadership.

"All right, enough already!" Matt said. "It's clear we don't know enough about Rifts to make decisions right now. They're rare, and none of us has ever run into anything quite like this before. We need more information. It's time to do some research. We should check out the Net, see what we can find out about them—safely, Andy!—and report back to the group."

While the others discussed which were the best places to start looking for answers, Matt blocked out the conversation for a moment. He couldn't forget the agonized look on Julio Cortez's face, and he just couldn't believe that pain was the result of a random program glitch *or* his own imagination. As the others bickered around him, Matt decided that something had to be done.

He had to be careful about who he asked to join him in his quest for the truth about Julio. He didn't know where a search for that truth would lead.

Matt knew that Mark Gridley would be a part of whatever happened next. Mark had been there when it started. But Matt also knew that he and the boy genius might not have what it took to get to the bottom of things, especially if international politics were involved.

It was important to take things one step at a time. . . .

And, Matt suddenly realized, the next step was right in front of him.

Matt raised both hands and called for order, and for a halt to the bickering.

"All right, shut up, everybody!"

The group fell silent. Everyone stared at their leader in this venture expectantly.

"You guys work on finding out more about Rifts. I'm going home to try to contact Julio in Corteguay," Matt said. "If I can talk to him, maybe this whole thing will be cleared up quickly and easily."

Mark Gridley nodded. Some of the others expressed agreement too.

"If I don't get the right answers," Matt continued, "we're going to have to take some kind of action. If Julio really is in trouble, we need to figure out a way to help him. Come prepared with everything you can find on Rifts and possible ways to work around them. We'll discuss our next move on Monday, after the competition against the Japanese students from Osaka.''

"At least we won't have to deal with Dieter," Andy Moore said.

David Gray nodded in agreement. "Yeah, he'll be fighting the Brits, changing the history of World War II."

"Don't get cocky," Megan warned. "I hear Masahara's Japanese are tough, too."

With that, Matt declared the impromptu meeting adjourned, and the group left the lounge, some to go home and head out into veeyar looking for answers, and some heading to their next summer course at the Institute.

Megan lingered behind, and approached Matt when the others had left the room. He turned and saw her.

"I could have used a little help there," he said.

"Oh, I thought you were doing just fine," Megan said, crossing her arms and tossing her hair. "I especially enjoyed the part where you zoned out. Good leadership management technique, Hunter. *Quirky*, but good."

Because Mark Gridley was staying at the Center for his weekly Thai boxing lesson, Matt Hunter caught an early autobus back to his home in Columbia, Maryland. Matt was actually glad to have this time alone.

He had a lot of thinking to do.

As the autobus pulled away from the huge interlocking geodesic domes that housed the International Educational Institute Center, across from the Smithsonian Museum of Air and Space, Matt wondered why his fellow Net Force Explorers were having such trouble buying into the fact that he and Mark had seen Julio in the simulator—and that Julio was in trouble.

In all the time he had belonged to the Net Force Explorers, Matt had done his best to make his friends proud—always. He'd worked hard, learned a lot, and had always demonstrated he was worthy of the trust Net Force had placed in him when they made him a Net Force Explorer. So had Mark Gridley, for that matter. Though the "Squirt" didn't get much respect because of his age, Matt was just as certain about seeing Julio inside the veeyar as Mark Gridley was. Yet the rest of the Net Force Explorers, including Megan, had not immediately believed what he and Mark were saying. They'd certainly agreed to help, but Matt could tell that not all of them were convinced that Julio and his problems were real. Some of the Net Force Explorers clearly still thought this was a simple machine error.

Why didn't they believe me? he wondered. *Why would I make up something like this? What would I have to gain anyway?*

Matt and Mark had no proof that anything other than a Rift had occurred, of course. All the evidence they had was locked up inside the veeyar's memory banks. But Matt still felt a little betrayed by the rest of the Net Force Explorers' doubt.

And without running through the program again, there was absolutely no way to prove to the rest of the world that he and Mark had really seen Julio Cortez. But they had, even though nobody believed them. And if Julio was really in trouble, Matt couldn't ask for help from anybody else, not until he had real proof. After all, if the Net Force Explorers didn't believe him, who would? Whatever the risk, and whatever the method, Matt was determined to discover the truth, and the evidence to support it. He had to—Julio was depending on him.

But right now, Matt had more questions than answers.

At least he knew what he needed to do first. He needed to talk to Julio. If he failed to contact his friend, for whatever reason, then he and the Net Force Explorers would combine their research about Rifts—find out everything available on what they were like, why they were dangerous, and what caused them.

In Matt's mind, Rifts still weren't real. The whole story sounded too much like the "laser rot" that his grandfather claimed was eating away at his collection of twentieth-century punk rock CDs—something else that Matt had always heard about but didn't believe actually existed.

Now a Rift was preventing Matt from helping one of his best friends, and he didn't like it one bit.

First Julio appears, then a Rift. Is it a coincidence? Not very likely, unless . . . ?

Suddenly, Matt sat up in his seat, his mind racing.

Unless the Rift had something to do with Julio's appearance! That was possible, wasn't it?

Matt sighed. He just didn't know enough. But at least he knew someone who could help besides Mark.

He needed to talk to his father. *Now!*

When Matt got home, he found two messages waiting for him. His mom had been sent on a mission for the Pentagon due to a sudden crisis, and his dad was stuck filling in for a sick colleague at an educational seminar.

I'm on my own for dinner, and I'm going to be alone for the weekend, Matt thought, disappointed that he could not speak to his father right away. *Oh, well, time for a snack.*

As he dug through the freezer looking for something to zap in the microwave, Matt remembered his father's virtual National Geographic Atlas.

When his macaroni and cheese was done, Matt took the plate into his room. As he began to eat, he stuck the two-inch-square South American datascript into his computer's drive, settled into his personalized chair, lined up the side-mounted computer neural interface that was implanted in his neck, waited until he felt the link take hold, and blinked a bit as he looked about his personal workspace.

Right now, in honor of the Net Force competition, it was set up like a control tower at a big aerospace port, and around the viewscreens that looked outward in every direction, giant airships took off and landed—each ship representing data that was interfacing with the Net.

Strapping himself into the command chair, he began to scan for information about Corteguay. It was like taking a voyage—although in virtual reality rather than in the real world. But the news he gleaned from his virtual trip was hardly reassuring.

Matt soon learned that calling Julio up on a simple video-phone was next to impossible. Most Corteguans didn't even have video-phones, just audio—and not very many Corteguans had those.

Worse still, direct communication between the "free world" and private citizens in Corteguay was tightly controlled. All calls into or out of the country went through government-controlled switchboards, and were routinely monitored or tapped. Mail was similarly censored. Communications with the socialist country were most often conducted through embassies or government agencies—less occasionally by private citizens or even businesses, though some of the sanctions against foreign capitalist ventures had eased recently.

If Matt wanted to talk to Julio Cortez, if would probably improve his chances if he went through the U.S. State Department. And it would take time. Hours, maybe even days . . .

That was a stunning revelation, a look into a world completely foreign and incomprehensible, and suddenly Matt Hunter was more sure than ever that his friend was in trouble.

But if it was going to be impossible to contact Julio on the Net, and tough to call him, just how *was* Matt going to talk to his friend and find out if he and his family were safe?

Well, he had a weekend to himself, enough food in the freezer to withstand a siege, and nothing but time on his hands. If there was a way to find Julio, he would do it. He wasn't a Net Force Explorer for nothing. Matt closed his eyes and headed out into the Net. . . .

Two days later, Matt sat in exactly the same place, though the litter of empty food containers around him testified that he'd at least gotten up for sustenance. He jumped when the incoming flight indicator went off, signaling that he had a call coming in on the Net. He brought the jet in for a landing. Mark Gridley's face filled his screen as he stepped out of the aerospace plane.

Mark was grinning like a Cheshire cat. He climbed down from the cockpit, tossed his hat to a waiting robot, and walked quickly across the tarmac and into Matt's tower.

"Are you alone?" Mark whispered conspiratorially.

Matt looked around the room in mock exaggeration, then faced his friend again.

"Yes," he said softly. "But we must hurry before this contact is traced."

"Don't laugh, Matt," the Squirt said with injured pride. "Because I got us in."

"In?" Matt said. "In where?"

"After Thai boxing class I went back to Dr. Lanier's office—" Mark didn't get a chance to complete that thought.

"Into the program?" Matt asked.

Mark nodded. "All we need is a cutting-edge system with enough memory and RAM to run the program—like the one in your dad's lab."

Matt's face paled. "I can't do that!" he said. "If the Institute traces the program to the point of access, my dad could get in trouble—maybe even lose his teacher's accreditation!"

"I've got it all fixed," Mark said. "Even if they trace us— which they probably won't—I've got a scrambler program in place. It took me all weekend to make it, but it's a beauty. Not even the CIA could track the origin of the call."

"Are you sure?" Matt asked, beginning to weaken.

"Don't worry about it," Mark said. "Who's the genius here?"

Matt said nothing, his mind in turmoil. Julio needed him, but his dad trusted him. There could be real and perhaps harmful consequences if this went wrong, for him and for his dad. And if he and Mark just yelled loud and long enough, they could probably get someone to let them go into the IEI program—maybe through Net Force or his mom's connections. But then Matt thought about Julio. If things were as bad as Julio said they were, delay could prove fatal for his friend and his family. And Matt had just spent all weekend proving that normal channels of communication were useless.

"We can get to the bottom of this—tonight," Mark said.

Matt thought about the look on Julio's face, about the things Julio had said, and he nodded.

"Good," Mark said. "I'll be at your place for real in about an hour."

The room went dark as Matt pulled out of his workspace and back into the real world. First, he got up and began to pick up the mess around his chair. After he'd thrown the cartons away and stuffed his dirty dishes in the dishwasher, he came back upstairs and settled into his computer chair. Matt sat there for a while, staring at the wall, wondering if he was doing the right thing.

By the time the doorbell rang, Matt had made up his mind.
He had to go through with this. He ran down the stairs to let
his friend in. But when he opened the front door, nobody was
there.

"If this is supposed to be funny, it's not working," Matt
said, his eyes searching the suburban street around his house.
He finally spotted Mark, standing to one side of the porch,
watching the little kids next door play soccer—or at least try
to. It would probably be a few years before they got it right.
Just now it looked more like the game was playing them. They
ran around after the ball in one big clump, trying to kick it,
but mostly getting in each other's way.

"You've come all this way—aren't you planning to come
inside?" Matt reached out and grabbed Mark's arm, pulling
him inside the house and shutting the door behind him. "So
now what do we do, hack into the Department of Defense's
war games computer and start World War III?"

"Chill, Matt," Gridley said. "This is not some movie or
the plot for a Larry Bond novel, you know. We're in absolutely no danger because nobody's going to trace anything
anywhere."

"How do you figure that?" Matt asked.

"Because there's no *reason* to," Mark said with a self-
confident smile. "We're not going to hack and crack anything,

because I've got the password. We're just going to knock on their door—with a nice scrambled phone line—and walk right in.''

Matt's eyes widened in disbelief. ''You really got Dr. Lanier's password?'' he said incredulously. ''How did you get hold of that?''

''It's not a state secret, you know,'' Gridley said. ''Dr. Lanier is a pretty careless guy. More than that, I cannot say.''

Matt breathed a sigh of relief. With a valid password and an untraceable phone line, they *should* be safe. . . .

''Now, take me to your computer,'' the Squirt said as he pulled a bulging backpack off his shoulders.

Matt led Mark Gridley down to his father's ''lab,'' which was a pretty impressive setup for an amateur. There were several research computers, about a thousand tools of all shapes and sizes, a bunch of unidentified electronic junk, and a computer-link chair. The Flight Simulation Museum at the Smithsonian and the simulators at the International Educational Institute used equipment very similar to the stuff in his dad's basement.

Matt Hunter's father, Gordon, was a high school science teacher. The school district supplied him with a top-of-the-line computer for his personal use, so he could review new educational programs at home instead of tying up a machine at the library or at school.

It was a nice perk, and his father made good use of it.

And so did Matt's mother. Though she now worked full-time at the Pentagon for the Department of Defense, Marissa Hunter was still listed as an active-duty fighter pilot, and she used the computer in her spare time to hone her skills when her busy schedule didn't allow her to get real ''in the flesh'' flight time.

The machine wasn't a toy, and Matt had only used it a few times before—and always with adult supervision. Upon reflection, Matt felt he and Mark were lucky that his father hadn't installed a security code to keep him from using the equipment when his parents weren't around. The computer in his room wasn't half the machine that this was, and who knew what kind of programs and stuff his parents had loaded on it. Matt knew they trusted him, and that made him feel even more ashamed of what he was about to do.

He kept telling himself it was all for a good cause, but still . . .

As Matt struggled with his conscience, Mark Gridley set to work. The youngest member of the Net Force Explorers was a veeyar whiz, and it took him almost no time to set up Matt's father's system to load the scrambler and set up a directory for the International Educational Institute's flight simulator. Now they just had to get that program.

With a bit of tinkering—and Mark's scrambler program in place and running—everything was ready.

Mark accessed the IEI computers over the Net. When he was in contact with them, he used Dr. Lanier's code to call up and download the Red Baron simulation—accessing the sub-files from that very afternoon and copying them into his father's machine, along with the program.

Now all they had to do was decide which one of them was going into virtual reality—as there was only one computer chair with a neural connection in this setup—then plug the lucky winner into the seat.

The decision was an easy one.

"You go," Mark Gridley said. "Julio's your best friend. I'll stay here in case something goes wrong—though I'd bet my bank account against a blown datascript that nothing *will* go wrong."

As Matt lined up his neural implant, Mark filled him in on the results of the call to IEI.

"I just downloaded two and a half minutes of the World War I program," Mark told him. "I figured we only needed the segment with Julio in it, and if there really *is* something wrong with the scenario, the less data we transfer, the less chance we have of grabbing the corrupted stuff and crashing your dad's computer. I'm also going to run a log of this as you go through the replay. That way, if the sim crashes after you get into it, at least we've got a record of what went on right up to the crash, and have a good idea of where we need to look to start fixing it. I've also programmed the sim to play from your vantage point. You were flying plane number one, right?"

Matt nodded.

"You should pop in close to the moment when Julio's tiger-striped airplane arrived. Everything should be the same as last time—unless the Rift has corrupted the data. Keep a close eye on the sim and see if you spot any differences from the first time you went through it." Then Mark smiled sheepishly. "You'll probably get in right at the moment when Dieter's plane got on my tail. Maybe this time I'll get lucky and do something right, huh?" They both laughed.

Matt was ready to go, and so was Mark.

"Good luck," Mark said, and activated the program.

For Matt, the transition from reality to virtual reality was always a little bit disorienting. One second he was in his father's lab, looking at his friend. The next, Matt was in his Sopwith Camel, flying over a veeyar battlefield in a veeyar sky, with veeyar winds blasting his face and making his eyes water.

The sensation was doubly odd because, as this was a replay, Matt had no control of his veeyar aircraft whatsoever. The plane, with him in it, followed the pre-ordained computer memory path of the events of the morning. Matt was just a passenger now, as he was when he rode on an autobus.

And it was a good thing too, because he didn't exactly have the attention to spare from his search for Julio or signs of a Rift to stay in control of the biplane.

Suddenly, ahead of him, Matt spotted Mark's Camel, with Dieter's Fokker Dr. 1 triplane in hot pursuit. Following its original path, the aircraft banked and turned toward the two airplanes. And as before, a German Albatross fighter crossed his sights, and the guns opened up.

As the other craft exploded, Matt could see the pilot wave at him once again, and blink out of existence.

While he gripped the sides of the cockpit, Matt's Sopwith Camel lifted its nose and turned into the path of the two approaching airplanes until they were facing one another head-on, just like before. When Mark's airplane raced past him, Matt found himself staring at Dieter's Fokker.

Matt's machine gun fired a single burst, then jammed as before.

Suddenly, the blue Fokker triplane's wing came apart, and Dieter Rosengarten's airplane spun out of control. But there was no sign of the orange, tiger-striped biplane that shot him down—nor was there any sign of Julio.

The veeyar skies ahead of him were completely empty.

As Matt's Sopwith leveled off, and flew parallel to Mark's airplane, he searched for Julio's aircraft. But where the tiger-striped plane had flown the first time, there was only blue sky and white clouds.

Then, as abruptly as the program began, it ended. Matt found himself sitting in his dad's mockpit, blinking in confusion.

Mark Gridley was staring back. "Well?" he said. "What did you see?"

But Matt didn't answer. He just stared at his friend with a look of profound disappointment. Mark's face sunk too when he saw the expression on Matt's face.

"I saw nothing," Matt said. "Not Julio, not even the airplane."

"Did you see a Rift then?" Mark asked. "A hole, an anomaly, anything at all?"

Matt shook his head. "My plane was there, so was yours and Dieter's . . . but no orange plane, no Rift, and no Julio," he said bitterly.

Mark sighed.

"Set it up again," Matt said. "This time I'll run the simulator and you hook up to the chair. Maybe you can see something from the cockpit of *your* biplane that I missed."

An hour later, Matt let Mark out through the basement door and went back upstairs. He and Mark had ridden the simulator three times each, and there was no sign of Julio locked in the memory.

Matt didn't know whether to be relieved or depressed by the results of their research, but he knew he was frustrated.

To Matt's surprise, his mother and father had come home while he was in the lab with Mark.

"Hey, Matt," his dad called from the family room couch. "What have you been up to?"

Matt shrugged his shoulders and said, "Stuff from my IEI class." To avoid the questions he was sure his father would ask next, he went into the kitchen to get a glass of milk.

Funny, Matt thought. *A couple of days ago, all I wanted to do was talk to Mom or Dad. Now I feel so guilty about using Dad's system without his permission that I can't even face them.*

When Matt arrived in the kitchen, he found his mom there, still in uniform, fixing dinner.

"If you're hungry, I made a nice salad," his mother said. "Fresh romaine lettuce with honey-mustard vinaigrette, and the lentil soup will be ready in a few more minutes."

If Matt *were* hungry, he'd rather have a hamburger and French fries, but before he could say so he heard his father calling him from the family room.

"Come quick, Matt," his dad said. "There's something on the HoloVid you should see."

Matt and his mom hurried out in time to catch the Sunday Night International Report on one of the twenty-four hour news networks. To Matt's surprise, the news anchor was doing a story about Corteguay's free elections and Ramon Cortez's bid for the presidency. Matt had missed the beginning of the report, but he knew he could access the whole story later on the Net if he wanted to.

". . . and in the Dompania district of Corteguay, opposition candidate Ramon Cortez campaigned in several rallies before large crowds. Though there is interest in the election, the greeting this former exile received in this heavily industrial region was less enthusiastic than the candidate might have wished. . . ."

On the screen, suddenly two-dee thanks to the stringent government control of the media in Corteguay, crowds of men in dirty overalls listened attentively as Ramon Cortez spoke from a podium. But there was not much enthusiasm on their faces, and no signs or placards proclaiming support for Cortez.

On the podium, an older man stood at Ramon's right side, and in the background, Matt spotted Julio standing with his mother, though there was no sign of little Juanita.

At one point in the broadcast, the camera panned across the faces of the Cortez family. Julio looked happy and excited, and Matt noticed that Julio was even wearing the jacket he'd won for taking second place at last year's Century of Military Aviation competition.

At one point, Julio turned and waved at a cluster of teenage girls in the front row of the crowd. As he did, Matt could read the glowscript words emblazoned on the back of the jacket. "Ace of Aces." A lot of people thought that was Julio's call sign, but they were wrong. It was *"Jefe"*—the Spanish word for "Chief." Mark's and Matt's call signs—WhizKid and Hunter—were much less imaginative.

As he watched the news story, a wave of relief rushed over Matt. *It was a Rift! A stupid, silly software glitch . . . I can't believe it.* But almost immediately, Matt's feeling of relief was replaced by the pangs of conscience.

He was determined to call Mark Gridley at his first opportunity and tell him about the broadcast. But there was one thing he had to do before that.

A very important thing.

Matt looked away from the screen when the story ended. "Dad, Mom," he said. "I have to tell you something, and I hope you won't get *too* angry. . . ."

"Well, I'm glad you told us," Gordon Hunter said when Matt was through confessing. His mother sat on the other side of the room, her arms crossed, silent.

Pondering my punishment, no doubt, Matt thought.

"You can bet that I'm going to put a security lock on that computer too," his father added. "If you were playing around with anyone else, I'd be even angrier. As it was, you were probably in better hands with Mark than you'd be with either me or your mother." Gordon Hunter looked into his son's eyes. "Which doesn't excuse what you did, I might add."

"I know, and I'm sorry," Matt said. "I was just so worried about Julio . . . it will never happen again."

"It surely won't," his dad said.

"But do you really think it was a Rift we both saw?" Matt asked. His father rubbed his chin and nodded.

"I'm pretty sure it was," he said. "You remember you were talking about Julio before he appeared, and Mark was part of the conversation. The Rift somehow triggered a random memory burst, and you both shared a hallucination—of sorts."

"But why did Dieter's Fokker go down, if we didn't shoot him down?" Matt said. His father shrugged.

"The software was defective," his dad speculated. "Anything can happen in a Rift."

Matt wanted to believe his father, and he guessed it sounded plausible, but he wasn't entirely convinced. *But still, there was that news story . . . I just saw Julio. He looked happy enough.*

As Matt listened to his father, he watched his mother quietly slip out of the room. He sensed that something had disturbed her, but Matt wasn't sure what. She was so cool under pressure, that fighter pilot's ability to roll with the punches was such an essential part of her character, that Matt knew it had to be something pretty bad for her discomfort to show.

While he and his father watched the news, Matt heard his mother bang around in the kitchen, probably ladling up bowls of steaming lentil soup from the autopot. But she never made that much noise unless she was really mad. Matt walked across to the kitchen and watched his mother, wondering just what was bothering her so much. He offered to set the table, and she didn't even look up.

Mom has seemed stiff and uncomfortable ever since I mentioned Julio, Matt thought as he put out napkins and silverware.

Matt's mother finished filling the bowls, and took them out to the dining room table.

"Come on, Matt, Gordon," she called into the family room. "Dinner's ready."

Matt and his father exchanged meaningful glances as they walked toward the table laden with vegetarian health food. Matt made a face.

"Don't worry. We'll sneak out for burgers later," his dad whispered.

As they all ate together, Matt continued to observe his mother. She seemed nervous and out of sorts, and didn't speak throughout the meal. His father noticed it too. And though she moved the food back and forth across her plate, Matt could see that his mother hardly ate a thing.

What's bothering her? Matt wondered.

On the other side of town, Megan O'Malley watched the same news story from the floor of her *dojo*. Some of the other students liked to spar on the sidelines with holo-dummies while they waited for their turn on the mat with the instructor, but Megan preferred to catch up with current events while she practiced her *katas*.

Today, she was working up a sweat running through some moves from one of her favorite martial arts disciplines, Pukulan Pentjak Silat Bukti Negara Serak, when the story came on the monitor above the practice floor.

Megan halted in the middle of a quick flurry of parries and ripostes to watch the news piece on the elections in Corteguay. But as she stared at the image of Julio at the rally, the tiny hairs on the back of her head began to prickle.

What's wrong with this picture? she wondered, confident about her own instincts for deception. She studied the image with a critical eye, looking for abnormalities of any kind.

Finally, she thought she spotted one, but the image passed too quickly for her to be sure.

Megan O'Malley already knew what she wanted to do when she was a grown-up. She wanted to enter the field of strategic operations, either for Net Force, the CIA, or the State Department. As the fifth and youngest child in a family with four boys, Megan knew the importance of planning ahead. It was the only way she could keep up with her sometimes-overbearing siblings.

Megan, a voracious reader, also knew enough about information management to know when someone was trying to manage her; and as she watched the rally in Corteguay, she got the distinct feeling that she and the rest of America were being had.

Megan promised herself that she would download the story and images from the Net when she got home that night.

When the news report ended, Megan returned to her practice. But her concentration was broken by the nagging feeling that there was something rotten in the state of Corteguay.

With a series of quick stabs, jabs, and blocks, Megan defeated her imaginary foe, pushed sweaty strands of brown hair off her forehead, and bowed deeply to her invisible nemesis.

First a shower, then I'm going home to watch that news story again. And maybe again and again after that.

4

By the time Monday morning rolled around, Mark and Matt had pretty much decided that they'd been misled by a glitch in a computer program. The entire episode in the simulator the previous Friday was a product of bad luck and their own vivid imaginations—taken to new levels with the help of a Rift, of course. Their experiences on Sunday—both the replay of the program and the news report from Corteguay—had left them convinced of it.

Though they both felt some tension and embarrassment over the incident as they rode to the Institute on the autobus for the next section of the course, World War II, they were relieved when none of the other members of the Net Force Explorers brought up Julio, or the Rift, again—with the exception of Andy Moore.

Andy continued to goad them about seeing "The Ghost in the Machine" until lunchtime.

But by the afternoon, after hours of practicing simulated takeoffs with P-40 Tomahawk fighters and listening to lectures on the politics and history of the world in the 1930's, all thoughts of the previous week were forgotten in the deluge of new information they had to absorb.

Finally, it was time for the first competition against the Boys' School of Osaka, led by Masahara Ito, the fifteen-year-old son of a financial consultant.

The scenario was called "Pearl Harbor," and perhaps understandably, things did not go well for the Net Force Explorers.

On December 7, 1941, as waves of Japanese carrier-based fighters and bombers streaked out of the sky to bomb the U.S. Navy base in Hawaii in a surprise attack that led to America's involvement in the Second World War, five young lieutenants had managed to take off in outmoded P-36's and P-40's from a small auxiliary field and carry the fight to the enemy.

Together, those five men inflicted more damage against the Japanese attackers that day than just about anyone else. And though the attack was a victory for the Japanese aggressors, the brave lieutenants who took to the air against impossible odds provided a much-needed morale boost for the U.S. military after the stunning defeat at Pearl Harbor.

Though the ten Japanese planes they downed were a paltry number, considering the size of the force they were up against, Matt and the Net Force Explorers would have loved to have done as well against Masahara and the Osakans.

Only one member of Net Force even got off the ground. In the first few minutes of the simulation, Matt, Mark, Andy, and David Gray were all shot to pieces as their P-40's lumbered down the runway in a futile attempt to get at the enemy.

Megan at least got her Tomahawk fighter airborne, but she was immediately attacked by a Japanese Zero. As Megan was going down in flames, she managed to swerve her stricken aircraft into the path of a Japanese dive bomber that had gotten too close.

It was the Americans' only kill that day.

Though their performance was terrible, word got out that Megan's suicidal retaliation had really impressed the Japanese team.

At the "debriefing" Dr. Lanier asked Megan why she'd rammed the Japanese airplane instead of bailing out.

"I got so mad when I saw the American ships burning in the harbor below that I just snapped," was her reply.

Even Andy Moore was impressed by that.

Later that day, things got even more intense as Dr. Lanier guided them through carrier takeoffs and landings in veeyar.

First they took off at the controls of single-seat Grumman

F4F Wildcat fighters, and then later in bomb-laden Douglas SBD Dauntless dive bombers.

The Dauntless was a two-seater aircraft, so the Net Force Explorers were paired up in teams: Matt as pilot in one plane, with Mark as his gunner; and Megan in a second aircraft, with Andy Moore as rear gunner.

David Gray was the lone man out, flying escort in a single-seat Hellcat. That was just the way he liked it.

The carrier takeoffs and landings had been intense, but the bombing runs were, in their own way, even more stressful. Matt couldn't believe how hard it was to fly a Dauntless and try to lob a bomb onto the target at the same time.

Matt concluded that flying one of these early World War II bombers was even harder than piloting a Sopwith Camel. Not one of the Net Force Explorers hit their target in four tries.

Things like that did not bode well for their next competition, and the classes ended early—without meeting the "enemy" in combat. The big day was Tuesday anyway, when the Net Force Explorers were scheduled to meet Masahara Ito's Osakans at a reenactment of the decisive Battle of Midway.

On Tuesday morning, after they watched some two-dee films of the actual battle, the Net Force Explorers were briefed by Dr. Lanier.

And then they were sent into veeyar.

As Matt Hunter was hooking himself up in the simulator room and waiting for his back seater to show up, Megan O'Malley approached him when the others were out of ear-shot.

"I want to talk to you after class," she said.

Matt nodded. "Sure. About what?" he asked.

But Megan moved away from him without acknowledging his question.

That's odd, he thought.

But Matt soon forgot about the mysterious exchange as he got back to the work at hand. Mark showed up finally, but he'd forgotten something in the briefing room and had to run back for it.

Matt's mind was spinning with all the things he had to remember, and he was glad that he and his teammates were "assisted" by user-friendly software that helped them with carrier takeoffs and dive-bombing runs.

In the simulator today, the Net Force Explorers were part of Lieutenant Clarence "Wade" McClusky's flight of Dauntless dive bombers, which launched from the deck of the USS *Yorktown* at 0925 hours—almost nine-thirty in the morning—on June 4, 1942, the second day of the Battle of Midway.

They were sent off to seek and destroy the Japanese carrier fleet, which was commanded by Admiral Nagumo from the bridge of the Japanese aircraft carrier *Akagi*.

Matt watched expectantly as the digital clock on the wall of the simulator room counted down . . . 004, 003, 002, 001 . . .

And suddenly Matt and Mark were in the cockpit of a weathered navy-blue Dauntless, loaded with a single thousand-pound bomb. They were on the swaying deck of the USS *Yorktown* in the middle of the South Pacific ocean on a clear, blue morning.

All around them, the dive bombers were lined up on the flattop's steel deck, waiting for their turn at the catapult.

"Here we go again," Mark said from his seat directly behind Matt. Both of their hearts were racing with excitement as they prepared to launch. With the cockpit open, the noise was deafening as dozens of fighters and bombers gunned their engines in preparation for takeoff.

Matt sniffed the air, and discovered it was rich with the scent of a wide ocean, tempered with the tang of diesel and oil fumes from the plane and the ship. Again, he was impressed with the details of the Institute's simulations.

A sailor signaled for them to move forward, and Matt carefully steered the airplane over the catapult rail.

A moment later, he was thrown back in his seat by the forces of gravity and inertia as the Dauntless was hurled from the tossing deck and into the bright blue sky.

"Go back!" Mark Gridley said. "I think I left my stomach on the boat. . . ."

Matt was too involved with trying to fly the aircraft to come up with a clever retort. If he stopped what he was doing long enough to be clever, he, Mark, and the Dauntless would be floating in the Pacific Ocean below them.

A few moments later, Megan and Andy's plane moved onto their wing, and David Gray appeared from above, the sunlight flashing off the glass panes of his cockpit. When the squadron was formed up, the aircraft headed toward the last known position of the Japanese fleet.

Thanks to time-compression, the Net Force Explorers spotted their target less than ten minutes later.

Matt recalled Dr. Lanier's history lecture. In the real battle, Wade McClusky's bombers had flown nearly to the limit of their range—about 150 miles—before they found the Japanese carriers. Finding the fleet that day was more dumb luck than strategic planning, but the lucky break turned the tide of the war in America's favor.

Matt also recalled that in the real Battle of Midway, the Japanese pilots were caught with their pants down. Their airplanes were all over the carrier decks, in the middle of being refueled and rearmed, when the Americans found them. And all that unprotected gasoline and all those unsecured explosives helped McClusky's squadron inflict real damage on the Japanese carrier fleet.

Suddenly, the simulated voice of Lieutenant Wade McClusky crackled in their headphones, ordering the dive bombers to attack the three carriers far below.

Matt banked his Dauntless and moved in for the kill, just five seconds behind Megan O'Malley's aircraft.

A bombing run in a 1940's-style dive bomber was a difficult proposition, and Matt's attack was strictly by the book. He lined his aircraft behind Megan's, and prepared to follow his wing*person* down to the deck.

Matt retarded the stick so that the nose of his aircraft lifted slightly, until it was above the horizon. Then he reached down and gripped the special handle between his legs, a diamond-shaped stick that deployed his dive brakes.

With the flaps down, the airplane executed a half roll, and nosed down into a seventy-degree dive. To Matt the plunge looked to be straight down, but if he checked the horizon every few seconds, he managed to stay oriented as to what was up and what was down.

Matt had a little more than thirty seconds to line up the yellow deck of the Japanese carrier he was aiming for in the crosshairs of his telescopic sight.

"Zeroes!" Mark said from behind Matt. "Right on our tail."

Matt didn't dare take his eyes off the target. "Keep them at arm's length," he told his tail gunner.

A moment later, he heard Mark Gridley's machine-gun fire, and felt the whole Dauntless shudder from the recoil. Then he heard his tail gunner whoop.

"I got one!" Mark said in triumph. Matt risked a sidelong glance, and saw the Zero spin toward the blue water.

"Good shooting," he said.

When Matt looked through his sight again, he discovered that he'd let the Dauntless drift. He moved the airplane back onto the target.

Meanwhile, the gunners on the carrier *Akagi* began to spray antiaircraft fire into the sky. Though their aim wasn't particularly accurate, a lot of lead was coming at the bombers.

Too much for Megan O'Malley.

As Matt watched, the wing of her navy-blue Dauntless sheared off when it was struck by antiaircraft fire. As her aircraft was going in, Megan tried to alert the others about her plight. But her cries of "Mayday" were cut off as she and Andy were dragged from the cockpit and back to reality.

The Dauntless spun into the waves, narrowly missing the crowded wooden deck of the Japanese carrier.

Matt was so low now that he could see sailors running about on the *Akagi*'s deck, and planes attempting to take off. He sneaked a quick glance at his altimeter. He was only 2,400 feet from the surface of the pacific, and the carrier was almost filling his telescope sight.

"Just another minute," he whispered to himself.

Suddenly, a Japanese Zero flashed past him, machine guns blazing. Matt felt his airplane shudder; then he heard Mark howl. The cry of his tail gunner was cut off suddenly.

"Mark?" Matt said. "Are you okay?"

But there was no reply from his backseater. And Matt had run out of time to worry about his friend. At exactly 1,500 feet, Matt grasped the handle on the bomb-release "pickle" with his right hand and pulled.

As the thousand-pound bomb dropped from the Dauntless's belly, Matt retracted the dive flaps and flashed over the deck of the Japanese ship.

Virtual sailors pointed at his airplane, and at the bomb plunging out of the sky right at them, and scattered.

As Matt tugged back on his stick, he felt the pull of gravity again. Then a bright yellow ball of fire exploded behind him, lighting up his control panel even in the harsh daylight.

Matt turned around in his cockpit in time to see the *Akagi*, Admiral Nagumo's flagship at the Battle of Midway, become a brilliant fireball that shattered the deck and tossed airplanes into the sea.

"Allll rightee!" Matt shouted, his backseater's fate forgotten in the rush of victory.

Suddenly, a familiar voice crackled in his headphones.

"Great shooting, man!" David Gray said from his Wildcat.

But in the seconds following the carrier's destruction, Matt had made a fatal mistake. Instead of jinking away from the explosion, dodging fighters and antiaircraft fire, Matt flew in an almost straight line, at an altitude of only about 1500 feet above the surface of the ocean.

He was practically inviting the Japanese Zeroes to attack him, so Matt shouldn't have been surprised when a couple of them accepted his invitation.

It was David Gray who warned Matt of an impending attack, just barely in time.

"You've got trouble coming," David said. "At your ten o'clock."

Matt twisted in his cockpit in time to see two yellow Zeroes streaking toward him. He knew he couldn't outrun them in the Dauntless, and he knew that Mark was out of commission. Without a tail gunner to fight back, Matt had only one option. He began to wiggle his plane back and forth in an attempt to dodge the bullets coming his way.

There wasn't much more he *could* do. The damage had already been done when he'd made the first mistake.

David Gray plunged out of the sky in a valiant attempt to rescue Matt, but his maneuver put him directly into the path of a hail of antiaircraft fire from the *Akagi*'s sister carrier, the *Soryu*.

The Wildcat disintegrated, its pieces striking the water and its shattered propeller skipping across the waves like a demented Frisbee.

Matt lifted the nose of his Dauntless into the sky, trying to gain some altitude. And the two Zeroes on his tail stayed with him. Matt knew it was only a matter of time now.

He heard bullets strike his Dauntless, and one of the dive flaps on his wing broke free, forcing him to fight the controls in order to stay in the air.

Virtual smoke began to pour out from under his engine cowling, and Matt knew he was a goner.

Suddenly, another aircraft flashed over Matt's head, so close to his canopy that he actually ducked. Matt twisted around and stared at the stranger.

His eyes widened in disbelief, and Matt gasped in astonishment when he saw another Wildcat fighter plane, this one painted orange from wing to tail and sporting black tiger stripes down its sides.

The Wildcat's wing-mounted machine guns blazed and one of the Zeroes exploded in a ball of fire and curling black smoke.

The second Japanese plane swooped low to duck under the Wildcat attack—too low, as it turned out. The Zero struck the wave tops and shattered into pieces that bounced across the Pacific.

Then a voice crackled in Matt's headphones. A familiar voice. A voice that Matt Hunter would recognize anywhere.

The voice of Julio Cortez.

Matt snapped back to reality abruptly. He blinked, not immediately aware he was back in real time.

Then Matt got his bearings. He turned and shouted at Dr. Lanier and the technicians.

"Freeze the program! Freeze it NOW!" he said. He'd pushed the button in his cockpit, but after his last experience with this problem, he was no longer sure that it was enough.

Matt was so agitated that he would have leaped out of his chair if he hadn't been belted in and hooked up to the computer. The Net Force Explorers hanging around the simulator room turned and stared at him in alarm.

Even Andy Moore, who was in the middle of accusing Megan of incompetence for getting them both killed, stopped talking when he heard the urgent tone in Matt Hunter's voice.

Meanwhile, behind the glass of the main frame's control booth, Dr. Lanier and another technician went into action, their commands filling the air in the attempt to snatch and preserve the program in the computer's vast data banks.

"What is it, Matt?" Mark Gridley said, rushing to the older boy's side. "What's wrong?"

Matt's eyes were wild as he turned to his friend.

"It's Julio!" he said. "He's inside the simulator—I saw him again!"

Fifteen minutes later, the Net Force Explorers were assembled in the ready room for their post-flight debriefing. Mark, Megan, Andy, and David were sitting in a cluster, separated a bit from Matt Hunter, who looked like he'd been through hell.

The debriefing should have started ten minutes ago, but Dr. Lanier was nowhere to be seen. Megan assumed that the professor was trying to determine what, if anything, was wrong with the Battle of Midway simulator program or the computer itself.

Across the aisle, Matt sat in one of the chairs, rubbing his eyes, while the others stole peeks at him from a safe distance. Mark Gridley approached and offered Matt a plastic bulb of ice-cold lemonade, which he gratefully accepted.

Mark met Matt's eyes. "You talked to him?" he asked.

Matt nodded. "Later," was all he would say.

Finally, Dr. Lanier entered the ready room, a computer technician in tow. He stepped up to the podium and apologized for being late.

"It looks as though we have a situation," Dr. Lanier said with obvious frustration.

"What exactly do you mean, sir?" Mark Gridley asked.

"I mean that we've discovered another Rift," the professor said. "This time it's in the Midway simulator."

"But that's impossible!" Mark said. "You said yourself

that Rifts are rare. How is it possible that *two* of them should turn up in the programs we used?''

Professor Lanier raised his eyebrow. ''How indeed?'' he asked suspiciously.

''You don't think *we* had anything to do with this?'' Matt Hunter said.

''I'm not accusing anyone of anything,'' Professor Lanier said. ''But I will say that the matter is under investigation, and I will say one more thing.''

He paused, letting the tension hang in the air.

''Someone accessed the Red Baron program on Sunday night,'' the professor said. ''The hacker was clever. He or she used my password to gain access, and covered his tracks . . . we couldn't trace the call.''

Dr. Lanier gazed out at them.

''I don't know if this is sabotage or some kind of sick practical joke, but until I find out, all simulations are suspended while we run a complete systems check.''

There were moans and groans in the ready room, but Dr. Lanier ignored them.

''That means Wednesday, Thursday, and Friday classes are cancelled. But unless you hear differently, everyone is to report back here for classes on Monday.''

The professor scanned the faces in the room one more time, and Matt and Mark were sure he was looking at them accusingly.

''That is all,'' he said, dismissing them.

5

"If you saw saw the haunted look on Julio's face, you'd believe me," Matt said to his teammates as they sat in the Net Force Explorers' Lounge, an area of virtual meeting rooms of various sizes filled with the results of their programming efforts.

"Julio acted as if he were suffering terrible pain, like it was difficult for him to even speak to me . . . He kept looking over his shoulder, like he was searching the sky for something that was after him . . . something that wanted to pull him back into his virtual prison cell."

"And you're sure no one else was in veeyar with you? Someone who might have seen his plane, or heard his radio broadcast?" David Gray asked from his chair.

He sat in the sun near a large picture window that, at this moment, offered a panoramic view of the Capitol.

Matt shook his head. "I doubt it," he said.

"I guess the pilots of the two Japanese planes that were shot down might have seen Julio's fighter," Matt added. "But if it's anything like the last time, then I'm sure they saw nothing out of the ordinary. Anyway, Julio probably hit both planes before they had even a chance to see him."

"Yeah," Andy Moore said. "Julio was an Ace, man! He always knew that the winner of a dogfight is the man who sees the other guy before the other guy sees *him*."

Mark Gridley nodded. So did Megan O'Malley.

Well, I've made some progress, at least. They're not looking at me like I'm crazy anymore, Matt thought. *Now they're discussing the possibility that Julio was in there with me. I guess that's a start.*

"What did Julio say to you?" Mark Gridley asked. "Tell us again."

Matt swallowed hard, then closed his eyes, trying to envision every detail of the harrowing scene in his mind.

"Well," Matt began, "I had the two Zeroes on my tail . . . and I had taken some hits already. My Dauntless was smoking, and Mark was gone. I knew that I was going down. It was just a matter of time." Matt took a deep breath and sat forward in his chair.

"Then suddenly, out of the blue came an orange Wildcat with black stripes," Matt recalled. "The pilot of the orange plane shot one Zero down, and the other one crashed into the Pacific trying to dodge his wingman's exploding airplane."

"But what did Julio *say*?" Mark repeated.

"I was fighting the controls, trying to stay aloft," Matt continued. "I heard Julio's voice over my headphones . . . I recognized it immediately. Julio asked me what day it was, and how much time had passed since the last time I saw him in veeyar. He said he was having trouble with his sense of time."

"That's understandable," Andy said. "If he's being held prisoner, they might be doing all kinds of things to him: sleep deprivation, torture, keeping him isolated, messing with his day-night cycles, or who knows what else."

Matt nodded. "I told him four days had passed, then I asked him how he got there."

"He slid his aircraft next to mine, right on my wing like he always did. And then he pulled the canopy back. . . ."

Matt paused. "I could *see* him, just as plainly as I can see you," he said. "Then Julio looked over his shoulder, like something was chasing him. I shouted to him, and I used his call sign to get his attention . . . '*Jefe*,' I called. '*Talk to me!*'

"He looked right at me then, and there was more sadness and pain on his face than I'd ever seen before. He spoke again, begged me to do something to save his family—to do it now, before it was too late.

"Then he said we weren't alone . . . that something was forcing him back."

"Something?" Megan asked. "Like what?"

"I don't know," Matt confessed. "Julio looked over his shoulder at that moment. Then his eyes widened, like he saw something catching up with us."

Matt paused again. "I think there was a shadow that passed over us, but I can't be sure. Then, I guess my Dauntless stalled or blew up or something, because the next thing I knew, I was back in the real world."

After a moment of silence, Megan rose and tossed her brown hair over her shoulder. She looked down at Matt, who was still slouched in his seat.

"I have some information that will help you prove your point, information that it took me a lot of digging to get. But first, before the details get fuzzy, let's go over this again," she said. "From the top . . ."

An hour later, Matt had gone through the events in the simulator time after time, but the Net Force Explorers were still no closer to figuring out what had happened than when they first arrived at the Net Force Explorers' Lounge.

But at least they now had a few theories.

"You know, Matt, I really think you were shot down," Andy Moore said.

David Gray rolled his dark eyes. "Not again, man," he muttered.

"Hear me out!" Andy said. "Right at the end, when Julio looked over his shoulder. I think he might have seen something coming."

"Like what?" Mark said.

"Like the thing he thought was chasing him," Andy said. "You admitted that you might have seen a shadow, right?"

Matt nodded.

"Well, I think you saw the shadow of the thing that was coming after Julio," Andy said.

Matt thought about it for a minute. "I guess I *could* have been shot down," he said. "But if I was, I didn't see it coming."

"We never do," David said softly.

"Of course not!" Andy said. "You didn't see the thing that got you for the same reason that the Japanese pilots probably didn't see Julio's plane, and Dieter never saw Julio's plane either: The attack came out of the sun while your attention was elsewhere."

"That *sounds* good," Matt said. "But . . ."

"Let's go with that theory for a second," Mark Gridley said. "It explains some things, but not others. Like why a Rift keeps forming while Julio is in the sim, and why there was no sign of Julio or his airplane when we played back the Red Baron program."

"Wait a minute," David Gray said, holding up his hand. *"You played back the Red Baron program?"*

"Oops," Mark whispered.

"Keep going, Squirt," Megan said. "Don't hold back now. The Holocat's already out of the veeyar."

Mark and Matt exchanged guilty glances; then they confessed all. They told the other Net Force Explorers about accessing the program using Dr. Lanier's password, and what they saw in the replay—which was nothing.

When they were done, it was David who spoke first.

"At least Dr. Lanier's mystery is solved," he said.

"If it wasn't for that Rift, we could replay today's simulation and go back inside," Andy Moore speculated.

But Megan shook her head doubtfully.

"I don't think so."

"What do you mean?" Mark Gridley asked.

"Figure it out, Squirt," Megan said. "When you pulled that program out of the computer's memory banks and replayed it, what happened?"

"We saw what we saw the first time, except for Julio not being there." Mark paused then, his face a mask of concentration.

"Yeah," he muttered. "Maybe we've been looking at this all wrong."

"What do you mean, kid?" Andy asked.

Mark stood up and began pacing as he explained his idea to them. "Maybe the Rift isn't causing us to imagine Julio," he said. "Maybe Julio is causing the Rift!"

"Huh?" David Gray said. But Matt and Megan were nodding.

"Those simulations are programmed to follow a pattern based on an actual historical event. Somebody has put the characteristics and appearance of all the equipment and all the battlefields and all the personnel of a given chunk of a war into the system—then arranged the pieces to reflect what really happened back then. We're given characters based on actual people carrying out actual missions, but whose actions we can control; still, most of the simulation is set up to follow a prescribed path. When Julio breaks in to communicate with us, he has to haul all the action off that path to buy the time to talk to us."

"And you get a Rift!" Andy said, finishing their thought.

The Net Force Explorers exchanged glances. They knew they were onto something. But suddenly Matt groaned.

"It's no good," he said.

"Why not?" Mark asked. "It all makes sense."

"It doesn't *all* make sense," Matt said. "I saw a news story a few days ago that featured Julio and his family. And I saw Julio. He looked fine."

"Any chance that it was an imposter?" David asked.

But Matt shook his head. "It was Julio," Matt said dejectedly. "I'm sure of it. Nobody could fool me about that."

"Don't be *too* sure," Megan said. "Wait here. I'll be right back."

Minutes later, Megan returned to the lounge with a two-inch datascript icon clutched in her hand. While the others watched her with mounting curiosity, Megan powered up the lounge computer and slipped the datascript icon into the machine.

Suddenly, a two-dee picture appeared on the monitor. It was the opening image of the news story about the Corteguay elections. The same one Matt saw aired Sunday night.

Right before the story began to unspool, Megan froze the picture. Then she turned back to her fellow Net Force Explorers.

"I saw the same news story you did, Matt," she said. "But I got the feeling that something was wrong with this picture. It took me a while to figure out what was going on, and then even longer to get the proof I needed to be sure I was right. Stick with me because this might get complicated.''

Megan gave a command, and the story continued to unspool. They all watched it to the end, and saw Ramon Cortez, his wife, and Julio on the screen. Only Julio's little sister, Juanita, was missing.

When the story was done, Megan reversed it and turned back to them.

''When I get out of school—*someday*—I want to go into intelligence work or strategic planning,'' she said. ''I want to manage reality the way most of you like to manage your veeyar games and programs.''

''What's a strategic planner?'' Andy asked.

It was Mark who answered. ''It's someone who develops strategies for managing people, situations, policies, popular opinion, stuff like that,'' he said.

''Close enough,'' Megan said. ''The important thing is that I know enough about the subject to recognize when *I'm* being managed. And who is doing the managing.'' She turned back to the flatfilm.

''Let's watch this story again, from the top.''

Megan played the story once again. But this time, she froze the picture on the very first images of the crowd watching the speech.

''Look at this,'' she said, pointing to the picture. ''It's a perfectly normal shot of a milling crowd, right?''

Everybody nodded. ''Now, supposedly, this shot was taken last week, in the Dompania region of Corteguay, right?''

Again, everyone nodded. Matt felt like he was back in school.

''But look at this.'' She pointed to the men in the crowd. They were wearing identical dirty overalls, like typical factory workers. A few of the onlookers were shielding the sun from their eyes with their hands. Megan pointed at them.

''It's pretty obvious from the shadows and the way they're squinting that these guys are looking into the sun, presumably watching the podium where Ramon Cortez is speaking.''

She fast-forwarded for a second or two. ''Now look at the podium itself.''

Matt could see that some of the men on the podium were

also shielding their eyes, as if the sun were blinding them too.

Megan froze the image. "Either the sun is in the eyes of the crowd, or it's in the eyes of the people on the podium. It can't be *both* places," she said.

"Sounds good, but that footage could have been taken at a different time than the first images," David Gray said, unconvinced. "The men could have been shot hours before the rally began."

Megan nodded. "You're absolutely right," she said. "This evidence, by itself, is inconclusive, but it got me thinking."

She turned back to the computer and asked it to fast-forward again. Then she froze on the scene where Ramon Cortez was speaking. "There's suddenly no sun in Julio's dad's eyes here—at least not in this shot." She moved the image ahead, one frame at a time, then zoomed in on a clock tower in the distance. She magnified the image until they could see the time, almost two o'clock.

But the sun was directly overhead, as if it were noontime.

"Of course," Megan admitted, "not every clock tower gives the right time, especially not in a poor socialist country where nothing seems to work very well."

Megan activated the picture again, and it continued to move ahead, one frame at a time.

"Socialists even manage to screw up their elaborate forgeries. Watch closely."

Suddenly, an anomaly that was hard for anyone to miss at this speed jumped right out at them.

"Did you see that!" David Gray said. "His tie changed color!"

"Exactly," Megan said, crossing her arms and looking at them. "I noticed that little glitch the first time I saw the story aired. It made me *very* suspicious."

Megan froze the picture again.

"After I downloaded the images, I put them through a digitizer and broke the picture up into its component parts."

As she spoke, she waved her hand at the computer and the picture split into pieces on the monitor, right before their eyes.

"If you ever wondered why Corteguay forbids holo-cams, it's because it's a lot harder to make fakes like this with holos."

She pointed to the images on the monitor again.

"This is a forgery," she said with conviction. "And not even a good one. The shadows are all wrong. The tie changes color, and there's sunlight reflecting off windows on opposite sides of the street at the same time.

"And look at this."

She zoomed in to focus on the plate-glass window in front of a store. "There's supposed to be a crowd outside this store, but the window is reflecting an empty street!"

David jumped to his feet and approached the monitor. Mark and Matt leaned closer too. Then they all looked at one another.

"It's a fake, all right," Matt said.

Megan nodded. "It's a fake, and *you* should have spotted it sooner, Matt!"

"Me?" Matt said. "Why me?"

"Because of this . . ." Megan gave the computer another hand signal and the flatfilm reformed and played on. When it got to the point in the story where Julio, in close-up, waved to a group of teenage girls in the front row, Megan froze the picture again.

"Look familiar?" she asked. Matt peered at the screen for a moment, then shook his head.

"Nope," he said. "You lost me."

It was Megan's turn to shake her head. "You disappoint me, Matt Hunter," she said as she gestured at the screen. "I thought you were smarter than that."

Suddenly the image on the screen moved to the left. On the right side of the monitor another image appeared. It was a news story aired last year, at the close of the Century of Military Aviation seminar, when the awards were given out.

Megan zoomed in on a shot of Julio Cortez, wearing his prized leather flight jacket, with "Ace of Aces" emblazoned on the back of it in glowscript. Megan froze that shot, then the shot from Corteguay. The two images were exactly the same.

"They stole that shot!" Matt said. "Julio wasn't at that rally at all!"

Megan turned to Matt. "You're right," she said. "But if Julio Cortez wasn't at the rally, then where *was* he?"

Suddenly, the mood turned very grim. Everyone knew the answer to her question, but only Matt dared to say it.

"In a virtual political prison, with the rest of his family," he whispered softly.

6

"We are trying to place a call," Megan said for the fourth time. "We want to speak to Mr. Ramon Cortez, in the city of Adello."

The operator on the other end of the line—a *human* operator, fortunately—spoke excellent English. But every time Megan mentioned Ramon's name, there was a long silence, followed by the operator's request to state her business once again.

"I am so sorry," the woman finally apologized after Megan explained everything to her for a fifth time. "We have no one listed under that name. Are you certain that this individual is actually in Corteguay?"

Megan snorted impatiently. "He's running for president!" she said. "Surely you've heard of him."

After a long pause, the woman told Megan that she would transfer her call to the supervisor. Perhaps he could help.

There were a series of clicks, then a dial tone.

"She cut me off!" Megan said, exasperated.

Matt, standing at her side, nodded. "The same thing happened to me all last weekend. I tried to call, but all I got was a runaround."

"I think it's obvious that the Corteguan government doesn't want us to talk to the Cortez family," Megan said.

"So what do we do now?" Mark Gridley asked no one in

particular. They'd pretty much exhausted the obvious things. A call to Net Force HQ had gotten them the news that Captain James Winters, the Net Force Explorers' liaison to Net Force, was out in the field on a special assignment and wasn't expected back for two weeks. They'd left an urgent message for him to call them, but hadn't heard from him so far. A call to the State Department with their news had been worse than useless—the man who'd answered the video-phone had told them to go back to playing with their dollies and let the grown-ups do the work. Repeated attempts to contact the United Nations had had almost identical results. The morale in the room after all these failures was not exactly at its highest point.

When Mark heard no reply to his question, he looked up.

Megan, Matt, David, and Andy were all staring at him as if they expected something.

"What?" he said.

"Why don't we take what we know to someone with real political clout?" Megan suggested.

"Like who?" Mark asked, obviously not liking where this conversation was heading.

"Yeah," Matt agreed. "Help may be just an autobus ride away."

"I don't know what you mean," Mark said stubbornly. But of course he knew *exactly* what his fellow Net Force Explorers were getting at. He'd already considered that same course of action himself, and then rejected it, for what he figured were obvious reasons.

"How about we all go see the head of Net Force?" David Gray asked with a pearly smile.

I knew it! Mark thought. But there was nothing he could do. He felt trapped as he scanned the other faces. Trapped and outvoted.

It was hard being the Squirt!

Going to Dad means admitting that I stole Dr. Lanier's password and used it without authorization, Mark thought miserably.

Matt Hunter could see the torment on his friend's face. "Come on, Squirt," Matt cajoled. "Confession is good for the soul. It was good for me."

"But it'll be bad for me," Mark said. "My life will be over

until high school!'' But Mark knew he was outvoted, and he also knew his friends were right. Finding out what had happened to the Cortez family was much more important than ducking any punishment meted out by his father.

Well, a little more important, Mark decided, dreading his father's wrath.

Mark again studied the faces of his friends, searching for an out. They were all looking back at him expectantly, waiting for him to make the first move.

"Okay, I surrender. Let's go find my dad." Mark sighed.

"I just want to say how proud I am that my son is a confessed computer criminal,'' Jay Gridley said, his face outwardly calm—though he was undoubtedly less than calm inside. He was fiddling with a pen as he spoke, and they could all see his knuckles whiten as he gripped it much harder than necessary. "I thought I taught you better, Mark."

Matt Hunter, Megan O'Malley, Andy Moore, and David Gray all stared at their feet as Mark received the quiet but firm rebuke from his father, who also happened to be the head of Net Force.

"You know, Mark,'' Jay Gridley continued. "You're the kind of guy I'm paid to catch."

"I said I was sorry, Dad,'' Mark said. "You don't have to *insult* me."

Matt Hunter, standing in the corner of Mr. Gridley's huge office and trying to act invisible, really felt for his friend. *He'd* confessed to using his dad's computer, and that had been embarrassing enough when he did it alone. He didn't want to think what Mark must be feeling as he fessed up in front of everybody.

"And anyway, Dad,'' Mark began.

Don't say it, Mark, Matt screamed to himself.

"I did it for a good cause."

Oh, no.

"No one ever does good by doing bad,'' Jay Gridley said. "And no outcome, no matter how positive, justifies a loss of honor to get there."

Then Jay Gridley scanned the faces of the other Net Force

Explorers gathered in the room. Only Megan and David Gray had the fortitude to meet the man's gaze.

And why not, Matt thought. *They didn't do anything wrong.*

Even Andy Moore, who wasn't a part of anything—*this* time anyway—couldn't look Mr. Gridley in the eyes. And Matt could see why. Though Jay Gridley hardly looked like an action HoloVid hero, he was a commanding and intimidating presence. His slender but powerful build radiated a physical and mental strength that few men possessed.

Matt had heard some of the younger Net Force recruits refer to Jay Gridley dismissively as "the Attack Hamster," but he doubted any of them could meet this man's gaze without wilting.

Dropping his pen onto the desk, Jay Gridley leaned back in his ergonomic neuro-chair.

"For now," he said. "I'm going to overlook my son's indiscretion in order to investigate the bigger picture."

As one, the Net Force Explorers breathed a sigh of relief.

"Are you going to seize the IEI flight simulators?" Megan asked. But Mr. Gridley shook his head.

"I can't," he said. "The International Educational Institute is the sovereign territory of the United Nations. We would need an incredible emergency and incontrovertible proof to justify such an action," he added as Megan started to interrupt. "Besides, with the elections in Corteguay scheduled and under U.N. observation, it would be all too possible for us to start some kind of international incident if Net Force gets involved officially. And if there's any public flap over this, your friend and his family would probably be the first victims. It's a lot tougher to get a straight story from dead witnesses than it is surviving ones. I'm sure the Corteguayan government would have a convincing explanation for the bodies. No, Ms. O'Malley, we're going to have to move carefully. Corteguay is a long way from here, and your friend's life might depend on our caution. If we startle those who are holding him captive before we're ready to act, there's no telling what they'll do."

Then the head of Net Force smiled the smile of a natural-born law enforcement officer. "Once we're ready, we can always cause a typhoon later, if we have to."

The Net Force Explorers all laughed, breaking, at last, the

grip of tension in the room. Matt laughed with the rest. He admired how smoothly the head of Net Force handled this situation. Megan often told him she learned more about what she wanted to be when she was a grown-up from just watching this man in action than she ever learned in classes. Matt too longed for the day when he could work alongside such remarkable and dedicated people.

"In the meantime, I don't want you talking about this to anyone who doesn't already know about it," Gridley told them all. "The fewer people involved at this point, the better."

He began to scan through his mail. "I'm going to make a few calls," he explained. "To the State Department, for one. The United States hasn't had diplomatic ties with Corteguay for many years, so the U.S. Embassy in Adello was shut down until fairly recently. It's still not officially open, though the U.N. is using it as a base for the election observers, and if the elections go smoothly, we'll be resuming official relations with Corteguay and installing an ambassador and staff. But I do know the former ambassador personally, and I intend to give her a call."

"What do you want us to do, Mr. Gridley?" Matt asked.

"I want you to return to the Institute on Monday as if nothing had happened, and continue your seminar," he told them. "I want you in those simulators, looking for any sign of Julio Cortez, or the virtual guard dogs that might be hunting him. And for heaven's sake, be careful." Mr. Gridley added, "You're Net Force Explorers. I know you'll do the right thing. . . ." The head of Net Force looked at his son meaningfully. "Now that you've all been reminded what the right thing *is*."

Mark Gridley nodded, and so did the rest of the Net Force Explorers. They were anxious to get back into the fray, and to save their friend if they could.

"Don't go quite yet," the head of Net Force said. "I don't want you going back into the veeyar sims without a little advice from an expert."

The head of Net Force gave a voice command to his computer.

"Contact Joanna Winthrop," Gridley asked. "Tell her to come to my office as soon as possible."

• • •

The Net Force Explorers knew Joanna Winthrop pretty well. She'd helped them out of tight situations in the past, and they hoped she would do it again this time.

Joanna was sometimes called "R"—it was a joke from some old twentieth-century two-dee flicks about a spy named James Bond. Bond's weapons specialist was called "Q." Joanna was called "R" because she was clearly a level above "Q." Net Force's weapons master was famous for coming up with better devices, and better ways to implement them in the cyber-world, than the bad guys.

But what the Net Force Explorers liked best about Joanna Winthrop was that she would rather hack into a heavily defended system or find a way to "debug" a computer infected with a deadly new virus than just about anything else.

That made her one of them, at least in the eyes of the Net Force Explorers.

In the past, Joanna Winthrop had been known to offer a new invention, or a program, or a datascript to the Net Force Explorers for their own personal enjoyment, like a high-tech doting aunt.

At other times, she'd provided the kind of high-tech devices that the Net Force Explorers needed to fix a problem, solve a mystery, or get themselves or others out of a bad situation.

Which was why the Net Force Explorers trusted her, and why they were glad to get her input on their current dilemma.

When Matt Hunter and Mark Gridley finished telling her of their experiences in the sims, Joanna Winthrop sat quietly for a moment. The Net Force Explorers exchanged uneasy glances during the long silence, wondering just what she was thinking. They were sure that Joanna Winthrop had never experienced a case like this one, and they wondered if she would believe them at all or—much worse—give them a fix any six-year-old should have come up with.

"I'm sorry to say that all I can offer is some theories, and a little advice," she said.

Matt Hunter saw the faces on the other Net Force Explorers fall. He felt disappointment too. But Matt recalled his father's words of wisdom. *Not every problem has a quick technological fix*, his dad had often said.

"Let's focus on exactly what happens in these simulations," Joanna said, interrupting Matt's thoughts. "According to what you've told me, it takes a little while for Julio to show up."

"Yeah," Matt said. "Usually in the nick of time."

"Let's think about that," she said. "It looks like Julio shows up and saves the day, but let's look at this another way."

"Like how?" Andy asked.

"I think it's got something to do with reprogramming the sim," Ms. Winthrop said.

"If that's it, why does Julio waste his time saving our butts?" Mark Gridley asked. "Why doesn't he just show up as soon as the simulation is activated, and tell us how we can help him?"

"Because when the simulator is first activated, he's got two problems. He has to break into the system and create or co-opt a character for himself," Joanna said. "Once he's got his character, he has to override the action programmed for the scenario and bend it to his wishes. He wants to communicate with you. The fewer enemies you have in the simulator, the easier that is for him to do. While you're fighting the battles programmed into the simulation, he risks getting hit and bounced back to wherever he is, for example, or having to find a new friend to communicate with if somebody comes screaming through the program and blows you out of the sky. So he needs to get rid of as many unfriendlies as he can. Even without potential enemies, I'd guess he's got a limited time to talk to you. The Rift eventually forms because he's using the system for his own purposes, overriding its programming and leaving it changed. But the less he has to do to it, the longer he'll have to communicate with you."

"Wow!" Matt said as the revelation dawned on him. "So if we go alone into the simulator, then Julio might be able to show up sooner and stay longer."

"Theoretically, yes," Joanna said. "But that doesn't deal with the problem of forming the Rift." She raised her index finger like one of Matt's high school teachers to stress her point. "And if you're right about virtual guard dogs chasing him, then the dangers of the Rift aren't the only ones Julio faces."

"Then what can we do to talk with Julio?" Matt said, his concern for his friend evident.

"As far as I can tell, your ability to bail out of the system at any time has not been affected during either of the two experiences you've had. From your descriptions, I don't think the Rifts that are forming are the kind to get anybody in trouble. So this might be dangerous for Julio, but shouldn't pose any danger to you. If things are out of control, get out of the game. Since this is virtual reality, not reality, you might get confused or upset, but you shouldn't get hurt. As long as you keep that in mind, you'll be fine. And Julio seems not to have any other choices open to him. It's clear he's willing to run the risks for the chance to talk to you. I think saving Julio is worth a little trouble, don't you? Go back to the Institute. Stay alive in the simulator. See what happens," Joanna said.

Matt and Mark looked puzzled for a minute; then it dawned on them both what she was getting at.

"You mean we have to win!" Andy said. Joanna nodded.

"You have to take out as much of the competition as you can. If you've eliminated the enemy, you should have time to really talk. So do your stuff and be there and ready to ask Julio questions when he appears."

Matt nodded, accepting Joanna Winthrop's theory. Mark looked determined. Andy looked ready for a fight. But David and Megan looked doubtful, as they remembered their previous dismal performance inside the air combat simulators.

"Don't think of the flight simulator battle as a harmless game," Joanna Winthrop told them. "Think of it as a war, because that is what it is. If you stay alive long enough, you'll win, and maybe even find a way to help Julio Cortez."

Matt Hunter rose, as he and the other Net Force Explorers prepared to leave Jay Gridley's office. But Joanna stopped them.

"Remember," she said, her eyes meeting Matt's, "if there really are hunters in veeyar looking for Julio, they are going to be dangerous to him. Be careful out there, and keep me posted."

7

As the ancient, American-built, four-wheel-drive Hummer bumped along the rutted, unpaved road, Mateo Cortez peered through the thick jungle vegetation. Though he knew that the complex was less than half a kilometer ahead, there was no sign of human habitation in this remote area of Corteguay.

Mateo had not visited the prison in the jungle since the day he had delivered his brother and his family to their jailers. But it was not pangs of conscience that kept him away; Mateo had long ago had any sense of guilt or shame beaten out of him by his master.

What kept Mateo away was the absurd but necessary farce of running his brother's highly visible political campaign. Almost daily he was in contact with the U.S. State Department, or an international journalist, acting the part of his brother's campaign manager. He refused all requests for interviews with Ramon Cortez, of course.

But with the world press watching Corteguay, and the Norteamericanos promising to send a former U.S. president to observe the election, it was too dangerous to shoot Ramon and his family, or even lock them in a cell and throw away the key.

It was much better, and smarter, to hold elections as scheduled, and make sure that Ramon Cortez and his opposition party lost by a wide margin. And that the party in power remained in power.

That way, it *looked* as if the people had spoken, but the current government still retained complete control of the nation and the economy. The party members also retained their secret Swiss bank accounts, their junkets to New York City under the guise of United Nations "fact-finding missions," and the other perks provided for the party elite.

It was a clever plan, and the bigwigs in Adello were impressed with Mateo for devising it. Mateo knew it made his master look good to *his* bosses, too. And since Mateo owed that man his life, he felt he had to repay that debt in some dramatic way. Mateo Cortez owed his master everything.

When the revolution had come to Corteguay, it was a poor country, with few assets, and though many in the current regime had thought then that it would be wise to put Mateo in front of a firing squad, one socialist party boss had thought otherwise, and Mateo had been spared.

He was tortured, broken, and brainwashed—but he was spared.

In the end, Mateo had proven to be an invaluable tool in the service of the socialists, as evidenced by the recent capture of his own brother and his family. When this was all over, Mateo would be rewarded for his loyalty. But that didn't matter to him.

All Mateo cared about was that his blood-debt to his immediate superior was erased forever. The debt paid in full.

For Mateo, that would be enough.

The Hummer rounded a sharp curve in the road and the driver, a lazy soldier with a stained uniform and a three-day growth on his unshaven face and neck, slammed on the brakes.

Instantly, a heavily armed Cuban exile clutching a rifle—not a stun gun, but a real weapon—rushed to let them in. As the wooden gate swung open, the soldier motioned them toward the main building.

The driver steered the Hummer to the low concrete bunker, isolated deep within the jungle, which looked exactly like a fresh-water pumping station—another ruse, this one to fool American spy satellites. As they drove through the gates, Mateo saw the sign on the fence, proclaiming the facility

''FRESH-WATER PUMPING STATION #16''—in Spanish, English, and Dutch.

Mateo also saw a half-dozen video surveillance cameras mounted on trees all around the compound. No one could move in or out of this place without being seen by the security team.

Mateo leaped out of the vehicle before the driver came to a complete stop. He pointed at the soldier behind the wheel.

''Wait for me,'' he said. ''I will be back shortly.''

As Mateo approached the single steel door on the square concrete building, it swung open. A technician in a white lab coat stepped aside to allow Mateo to pass.

''The commander wants to see you immediately,'' the technician said.

Mateo grunted. *Of course he wants to see me, you ass,* he thought. *I wouldn't have come at all if that were not the case.*

Inside the low building the temperature was cool. Air-conditioning was vital for the delicate computers to run at peak efficiency. Mateo felt a chill. He crossed the room and stood before a second steel door.

''Name,'' a distorted electronic voice said from an invisible speaker.

''Mateo Cortez,'' he said, staring into the retinal scanner mounted above the door. A moment passed, then the lock clicked, and the heavy door swung open automatically.

''Pass,'' the electronic voice said.

Mateo entered the elevator, which instantly plunged over a hundred feet, taking him to the main holding area deep underground.

Mark Gridley sat silently—as per instructions—in his father's office at Net Force headquarters. He was listening with mounting anger to his father's guest talk about him as if he wasn't even there.

Jay Gridley was meeting with Walter Paulson of the State Department. His dad had told Mark before this meeting that Paulson had been a career diplomat for fifteen years, ever since he'd graduated from Harvard and passed the diplomatic corps exam. Mark knew, thanks to his father, that this man had handled a variety of political crises. Mark also knew that Paulson was dismissing the Net Force Explorers' story about Julio out of hand. He could see the skepticism on the career diplomat's face as Paulson spoke to his dad. He could also see that his father's anger mirrored his own. Though it was difficult, Mark Gridley kept quiet as his father argued with the man.

"You're telling me that the State Department is unwilling to stick its neck out to get to the truth?" Jay Gridley said, his face a mask of outrage.

Walter Paulson sighed.

"I did not say that, Mr. Gridley," Paulson said. "I merely suggested that the State Department wasn't ready to risk what few diplomatic channels we have in Corteguay on a wild story told by of a bunch of teenagers."

That last remark made Mark Gridley wince, but he still kept silent.

"Are you suggesting they made it up?" Gridley said.

Again, Paulson shook his head, his calm exterior unruffled. "I am suggesting that they may be mistaken, or this may be a childish prank. . . ."

"A prank!" Jay Gridley said. "My son, the boy you see sitting right there, is one of those 'teenagers' you so quickly discount, Mr. Paulson. He is not the kind of kid who pulls pranks."

You tell him, dad! Mark thought.

Walter Paulson cleared his throat. "Well, naturally, as his father—"

"As his *father,* I trust my son, Mr. Paulson," Gridley snapped back. "And I think that something is wrong in Corteguay!"

Walter Paulson sighed again. "Mr. Gridley," he said calmly. "I want to assure you that the State Department is monitoring the elections in Corteguay very closely. Former President Daniel Tucker will be traveling to the capital city of Adello for the actual election, and we have been in almost daily contact with Mateo Cortez, the opposition candidate's brother. . . ."

The career bureaucrat paused before continuing.

"Rest assured, Mr. Gridley. We are doing everything in our power to guarantee that there are safe, honest, and free elections in Corteguay,'' Paulson said with authority, his eyes meeting Mark's for the first time.

''Wild stories of virtual concentration camps for political prisoners are nothing more than a figment of a child's over-active imagination. You have my word on it.''

The seven prisoners were lined up in a neat row, each strapped to a separate implant table topped by a stained ergonomic vibro-mattress. All of the prisoners were naked, though they were each nearly covered by a blanket and a complicated-looking electronic helmet that hid their eyes and ears. Thick electronic cables were also plugged into their subdural implants.

In one corner of the room, a fat, slovenly woman in a stained white dress and hemp sandals sat on a stool. A pan of soapy water and a sponge sat on the floor at her feet.

She was there to provide for the prisoners' ''physical needs,'' which meant that she cleaned them up occasionally. But not thoroughly or often enough, Mateo judged from their appearance.

Circling the line of tables, Mateo gazed at the prisoners dispassionately. Though he had been a prisoner himself, he felt no empathy for these hapless victims of the cruel regime.

He noted that the ergonomic mattress repositioned them at pre-set intervals so that the prisoners would not get bedsores from lying in one position all day. Mateo also saw that they were being fed. The prisoners all had feeding tubes inserted into their nasal passages and were receiving some sort of so-lution—probably a mixture of water, electrolytes, and the drugs that kept them unconscious and mentally submissive to the computer link—intravenously through needles in their arms. Other tubes eliminated their body waste, dumping it into containers situated under the implant tables. The stench was appalling.

Occasionally, one of the prisoners would twitch. Otherwise, they showed no sign of life other than their steady breathing and the drip of the IVs.

And the odor.

Mateo unconsciously reached up and covered his nose.

"I suspect you are wondering why I summoned you here, Mateo," a familiar voice said.

Mateo Cortez turned and faced his master. He fought the urge to salute, which was quickly followed by an almost uncontrollable urge to flee. It was an impulse he'd never lost from those endless months of mental and physical torture that he had experienced at this man's hands.

Mateo merely nodded, but as his master gazed at him with cold eyes, he felt as if his torturer understood Mateo's psychological reaction perfectly. The man no doubt took pleasure in it.

"It has come to my attention that there has been a temporary escape," the man said. Mateo turned back to the prisoners, counting.

"Escape?" he repeated. "They are all here. How can they escape?"

"Through the Net," his master said.

Mateo's eyes widened in surprise.

"Fortunately, I planned for this possibility," his master said.

"Who was it?" Mateo asked.

"The boy, Julio," the man said. "He is very resourceful for one so young. A credit to your family. Perhaps I will have the chance to break him and make him my own. I look forward to it. After the election, of course."

Mateo shuddered, and feared his master had seen the involuntary movement.

"Fortunately, the autoguards caught him and brought him back to us," the master said. Mateo's weakness had apparently gone unnoticed.

"Then this will not happen again?" Mateo asked.

"On the contrary," the master said. "It *will* happen again. I will *encourage* it to happen again. I want to know how the boy did it in a system that has no access to exterior phone lines or hard-wired connections to the Net, and I want to know where the boy went and who he communicated with, so that those persons can be dealt with, too."

"Assassins," Mateo said. His master nodded.

"*Virtual* assassins, Mateo . . ."

•   •   •

Lieutenant Commander Marissa Hunter walked briskly down the long corridor, her low heels clicking on the slick floor. She was passing through the operations wing of the Pentagon, a high-security area monitored and closely guarded at all times.

She had been here often in the last few months, since she'd been transferred from active carrier duty to an advisory position in the U.S. Navy Special Operations Command. It was an important job and good for her career, but Marissa Hunter was an aviator first and foremost and she missed flying the hot fighter planes she loved.

That was not saying her desk job had been boring—far from it.

During her time at the Pentagon, Lieutenant Commander Hunter had been asked to review and evaluate over a dozen special operations scenarios, with the understanding that everything she read and learned was to remain top secret. The data was never to be discussed again, with anyone, unless her expertise was once again requested by her superior officers.

In essence, she was expected to read, evaluate, and then forget what she learned.

Forever.

But ever since her son had told her a seemingly wild story about seeing his best friend trapped in veeyar, claiming to be a political prisoner in his native land, memories of an operation she'd reviewed a few weeks ago came back to haunt her.

Operation Raptor.

Lieutenant Commander Hunter knew she shouldn't even remember the code name. And right now, she wished more than anything that she'd never heard of Raptor, or of Colonel Max Stegar, the man in charge of it.

But it was too late for regrets, Hunter knew. She'd already "bitten the apple," as her husband was fond of saying.

As she thought about her family, Marissa Hunter slowed her pace, still torn by doubt about what she was about to do. *Am I doing the right thing?* she wondered.

Lieutenant Commander Hunter paused in front of an office door. She looked up and saw Max Stegar's name plate on the door.

If I knock on that door, there'll be no turning back, she thought grimly.

Then she took a deep breath . . . raised her hand, and gave the door a couple of sharp raps.

"Come in," United States Marine Corps Colonel Max Stegar said when he heard the knock. His voice was gruff as he looked up from the paperwork spread across his desk for the first time that morning.

The door opened and a female Navy officer walked in and saluted smartly, signaling that this was an official visit.

Stegar returned the salute. *That's Marissa Hunter,* he recalled. *The Naval aviator who helped to plan the evacuation phase of our upcoming operation.*

The Marine officer decided he'd better listen to what she had to say.

"What can I do for you, Lieutenant Commander Hunter?" he asked.

"Permission to speak off the record, sir," the woman said.

Stegar threw his pen on the desk and frowned. "There is no 'off the record' in my office, Lieutenant Commander," Stegar said. "Speak your piece, or leave now and I'll forget you were ever here."

"Then, permission to *speak,* sir."

"About what, Lieutenant Commander?" Stegar asked.

"About a possible special operation that might currently be in the planning stages, sir." She met his eyes squarely as she said that.

"You *are* aware that you're not supposed to discuss special operations once they are beyond the preliminary planning stages, aren't you?" Colonel Stegar asked.

"But I have new information, sir," she replied without missing a beat.

"New information about what?" Stegar asked.

"About Raptor, sir," she said.

Colonel Stegar's jaw tensed. "All right, you've got my attention. Tell me what you know."

And so Marissa Hunter took a deep breath and told him about her son's on-line adventures with his young friend Julio Cortez, and his conclusions. As he listened to the wild story, Colonel Stegar's gut tightened. Scattered among the trappings of a tale that would do a speculative-fiction writer proud, he found a few elements that verified hard-won military intelligence in Corteguay. Those elements made him wonder if there wasn't something here he should listen to. The matter was one of considerable importance to Stegar. He would be putting his life, and the lives of his men, on the line in Corteguay in the very near future.

After she'd finished, the Navy officer stood in front of Colonel Stegar and waited for his reaction.

He sat silently, wondering what he should do next. He thought about what he should—what he could—tell this woman. Her security clearance was high enough to tell her everything, and that was finally what he decided to do. He owed it to his men to utilize every resource at his disposal. "We're in the process," he began, "of an evacuation operation for several United States citizens currently being held captive in Corteguay. Seven months ago, two retired military personnel—one of them a former Navy SEAL—accompanied an overzealous Christian missionary into Corteguay's jungles." Stegar activated a map-table inset in his desk's surface.

"They sailed in and anchored here"—he pointed out the location—"in an unoccupied cove far from any human settlements. They hid the boat, and moved inland southeast through Corteguay's rain forests."

On the flat horizontal screen, a map of Corteguay was projected over real-time images of the country itself, beamed continuously by spy satellites to computers in the Pentagon. The two images, with dark borders and geographical names over the real-time projection, meshed perfectly on the map screen.

"Dr. Price, the missionary who led the expedition, had heard rumors that a tribe called the Huertos was being persecuted by the socialist regime in Corteguay," the colonel continued. "Price and the two others were captured, of course."

"Sounds like they knew what they were getting into," Lieutenant Commander Hunter remarked.

Stegar nodded. "They put their own fannies into the fire, that's a fact," he agreed. "But there are . . . complications. The SEAL with the group was a former anti-terrorism specialist. Colonel Breen was good at what he did, and in his day he formed many cells within some of the worst terrorist groups active today—The Shining Path, Cuba Libre, the Palestine Liberation Organization, the Jewish Defense League, you name it. The names and faces of those spies are locked in Breen's head.''

''What was he doing there then?'' Hunter asked.

''He found religion,'' Stegar replied. ''I can't fault him for that.''

''So Raptor's a plan to get him out, along with anybody else you can grab,'' she said.

Stegar nodded. Then he waved his hand over the map station and the image shifted and magnified, until they were looking at another spot on Corteguay's coast, about fifty kilometers from Adello, the nation's capital.

''The men were brought here,'' Stegar said, pointing to a magnified image of a primitive prison on a jetty of rock jutting out into the chasm of a river basin.

The buildings were made of wood and tarpaper, the fences were mostly barbed wire—though a code in one corner of the map station indicated some of them were electrified. The details of the real-time images were so clear that Hunter could see men in ragged clothes moving around in the yard and near the latrines, and armed guards in the towers.

''In less than a week, we're going in to rescue those men,'' Colonel Stegar said. ''The mission was green-lighted when we learned that Ramon Cortez and his family are also being held in this camp.''

Marissa felt a pang of apprehension. So much could go wrong. Though she'd flown her share of missions to support men like the ones who would extract the prisoners, special ops were too out of control for her tastes, too dependent on chance and the lay of the land. She always wondered how men like Colonel Stegar did it on a regular basis. No wonder this Colonel Breen had found religion.

''We've modified the plans slightly since you saw them. We'll arrive underwater, then move inland along the river,'' the colonel continued. ''SEALs have already deactivated the coastal defense—though the Corteguans don't know it yet—and once we're there we'll take out these guard towers. It's all by the book. The prisoners are in this building.'' He pointed to a shack not much different from the others. ''We'll be in and out before the security forces even know about it.''

"But I don't see how these shacks could hold a veeyar installation," Marissa said. "The individual buildings don't even have power, and I don't see any technicians.''

Colonel Stegar looked up from the table, straight at her.

"I'm sorry, Hunter, but I can't buy your son's story. It's just too Larry Bond for my taste. The Corteguan socialists are brutes, not technicians.''

"Then how do you explain the fact that Matt knew that Julio and his family had been taken prisoner? My son was absolutely right about that, and it's hardly common knowledge.''

"I'm willing to allow that your son got a message of some sort from his friend. I just don't think the boy got his details straight about where they're being held," the colonel said.

Marissa Hunter clearly didn't believe her son could be mistaken in what he'd seen and heard. She scanned the map, looking for another possibility. Finally, she spotted something a few kilometers away, a low concrete building with two or three outbuildings, one next to a propane tank with electrical lines fanning out from it—clearly a power generator of some sort, and a water tower with a small parabolic dish antenna mounted on top of it and a pump next to it.

"What about this?" she asked, pointing.

"Insignificant," Stegar said, shaking his head. "A Dutch-built electronic fresh-water pumping station. The Corteguans can't afford desalinization technology, so they pump deep water up from underground. The pump works without a crew and hardly anyone ever goes there.''

"If the station's unmanned, why does it have a communications antenna stuck on the water tower?" she asked.

"It's the tallest structure, man-made or otherwise, around there—has to be, to build enough pressure to run fresh water all the way to the capital city, Adello. Also, the station's where the electricity, what there is of it, that they use at the prison camp is generated. It makes sense to mount an antenna there. But we've been watching, and the place is deserted almost all of the time.''

But as she gazed at the real-time image, Marissa Hunter saw a military-looking vehicle parked right outside the central structure and a soldier loitering nearby. Colonel Stegar saw it too, but said nothing.

"How do you *know* they're in that prison you're pointing at, Colonel?" she asked.

"Humint, Lieutenant Commander," he said. "Human intelligence . . . we have a mole in the Corteguan government."

"Do you trust that agent?" she said.

Stegar nodded. "He's a native, and an insignificant member of their economic council. A man named Manuel Arias. We trust him."

Marissa looked away from the map, and back at the colonel. "So this has all been cleared?" she asked.

"By the president himself," Stegar said. "The State Department is in on it, too. They know Cortez and his family have been grabbed, but they're not going to admit it to anyone, not until Operation Raptor is completed."

Ten hours later Colonel Stegar was still at his desk. "Come in!" he barked, annoyed at getting interrupted yet again. As the time for the mission called Raptor rapidly approached, more and more details had to be in place, and more things had to be set into motion. Like the dinosaur the mission was named after, Raptor threatened to get out of control and eat them all alive.

Colonel Stegar had been at it for twelve hours straight, living on coffee and nutri-bars. He was beginning to feel the strain.

The door opened and a young lieutenant entered and saluted. "I have your new sitrep, sir," the Marine said.

Stegar returned the salute and motioned the man forward. The young lieutenant handed the grizzled, battle-hardened colonel the situation report. There were red plastic tags on several pages of the hardsheet.

"What's this?" Stegar asked, pointing to one of the tags, on the first page of the hardsheet document.

"You requested a report on any change of activity around Oz, sir," the lieutenant said. "There has been some activity."

Oz was the code name for the prison in Corteguay where the hostages were being held. Stegar didn't need complications, but apparently he had them. The colonel scanned the report, then dismissed the lieutenant.

As the young officer departed, Colonel Stegar sank back into his chair. According to the hardsheet intelligence report, there had been increased activity at the nearest human settlement to the prison—at a Dutch-built fresh-water pumping station. Number 16, according to intel.

Trucks and cars were coming and going, and at least five men had been spotted by satellite outside the concrete bunker at one point earlier this morning.

He looked at the stillshots. One of the men was wearing a white lab smock. A few more were carrying boxes that looked suspiciously like computer equipment.

Stegar sighed. He recalled Lieutenant Commander Hunter's remarks about that pumping station, and her son's wild theory that a secret computer center was holding his friend Julio prisoner, one that his mother felt was housed inside that innocent-looking concrete bunker.

After this stillshot, Colonel Stegar was beginning to wonder if the theory was so wild after all. He dropped the report on his desk and rubbed his tired eyes. He had a sinking feeling that he wouldn't be getting much sleep any time soon. In the next few hours he was going to put into motion an operation that had to be carried out flawlessly or people would die—lots of them, himself included—and his government would be embarrassed. And he still had to choose his target. He had a choice of two targets now—one based on the very best information that military intelligence and a trusted internal source in the Corteguan government could give him. The other choice was based on the testimony of a teenage boy who'd never set foot in Latin America, who claimed he'd learned of it while playing in a virtual reality competition.

Picking the invasion site was Stegar's choice to make, and the success or failure of the operation depended on it.

He knew, of course, which was the logical choice.

Taking a deep breath, he selected the target for the rescue operation. May God have mercy upon all of them if he was wrong.

· · ·

"I can't believe what I'm hearing," Matt Hunter said.

The Net Force Explorers were sitting around in their Virtual Lounge. This was usually the time for their weekly meeting, but school was out and so many of their members were on vacation with their families or on a school-sponsored virtual field trip to Zaire that Matt, as president of the Washington, D.C., area Net Force Explorers chapter, had called the meeting off.

That was when Mark Gridley showed up and gave them the bad news.

"Why *can't* the State Department do something?" David Gray asked. No one could answer him.

"You know," Andy Moore said, "Julio's parents weren't U.S. citizens, technically. They were political exiles who kept their Corteguan citizenship."

"But America is supposed to *stand* for something," David shot back. "We have interests in the region."

"And anyway," Matt added. "Julio's little sister, Juanita, *was* born here. That makes *her* an American citizen at least!"

"Bureaucrats really make me sick," David said, his head resting on his hand.

"Yeah," Matt agreed. "My dad says that the State Department's always been sympathetic to socialist governments. The diplomats feel they're more stable for political purposes than a democracy."

"Maybe we should go public," Andy Moore said with a devilish grin. His idea brought objections from practically everyone, especially Mark.

"Don't forget what my dad said," Mark said. "Julio could be in danger if we blow the lid off this. We're supposed to keep quiet about what we know."

"What good is *that* gonna do?" David asked. "It only plays into the Corteguan government's hands."

"Wait a minute," Megan O'Malley said. "We've got to stick to Mr. Gridley's plan," she said. "Monday is only a few days away. When we get back into those flight simulators, we'll get some answers."

"But what do we do in the meantime?" Andy said.

Matt Hunter and Mark Gridley exchanged glances. Then Mark spoke.

"I know what *I'm* going to do," he said.

"Me, too," Matt said.

All eyes turned to the two of them.

"What?" Megan finally bit.

"I'm going to the flight simulator down at the Smithsonian and book some practice time," Matt said with conviction.

Andy, David, and Megan exchanged glances too.

"Let's go," Megan said, leading the way.

8

Monday morning came much faster than any of the Net Force Explorers thought possible. That was because they'd spent hours every single day in the Smithsonian's Flight Simulator Museum, practicing their maneuvers in World War II aircraft so that they could increase their chances of surviving the competition.

Matt realized that a major problem they were having in their previous encounters was caused by the fact that the Net Force Explorers were acting like a bunch of individuals and not as a team. He and Mark had lasted to the end of the Red Baron simulation because, as Mark's wingman, Matt went out of his way to protect his partner.

Everybody else, it seems, was out to prove something on their own. Especially Andy Moore, who had a personal grudge against the leader of the German team.

Now, with a single group goal that was bigger then their own concerns, the Net Force Explorers were behaving more like a cohesive unit. Even Andy Moore stuck to the program. While in the simulators anyway.

He was still clowning around and getting on David Gray's nerves the rest of the time.

Of course, they had been told by people who'd used both that compared to the Institute's simulators, the sims at the Smithsonian were less detailed, less realistic, and a bit easier

on the pilot. Despite this, after flying a dozen flights at the
Smithsonian, David said that flying the P-51 Mustang was so
effortless that he thought his grandmother could do it. Matt
hoped David was right. But the Net Force Explorers were there
to hone more than just their flying skills. They needed to learn
to fight as a team, to learn theory, and to learn to communicate
better under combat conditions.

By the time they stepped out of the autobus in front of the
Institute on Monday morning—all of them together, as a
team—the Net Force Explorers felt they were ready. If they
failed now, at least they'd done their best.

Dr. Lanier was almost jovial when he entered the classroom
that morning. He informed the Net Force Explorers that a
check of the entire computer system had been performed over
the weekend, and the simulators were up and running perfectly, with no sign of the Rifts that had been plaguing them.

Lanier made no mention of the illegal access of the program
the week before, to everyone's relief.

So after a quick introduction to the legendary British fighter
of the Second World War, the Spitfire, the Net Force Explorers
were ushered into a non-interactive TeacherNet program about
the Battle of Britain.

Through a dramatic series of slickly compiled and edited
holo-images, the Net Force Explorers learned about the events
leading up to the Battle of Britain—the first-ever battle fought
exclusively in the air, with two of the twentieth century's
greatest European military powers, Great Britain and Nazi
Germany, struggling for superiority in the skies over England.

The TeacherNet program began by taking the Net Force
Explorers on a virtual tour of the early days of the Second
World War.

First they were dropped into the crowd at a Nazi rally,
where they learned of Adolf Hitler's plan to conquer Europe.
Another jump took them to that fateful morning of September
1, 1939, when German troops launched their blitzkrieg—
"lightning war"—against Poland, starting a conflict that
would rage for six years.

The Net Force Explorers ducked for cover as German
fighter-bombers swooped out of the sky, destroying Polish
military facilities. Then, from the cockpit of a German Heinkel

He-111 bomber, the Net Force Explorers watched as Poland was decimated.

Another jump took them to the ground again, where they observed streams of Germans fighting against valiant but outgunned soldiers of the Polish horse-mounted cavalry—who were easily defeated by the Nazis' superior technology.

The parade of images took them next to June 1940. The Net Force Explorers listened to the speech given by British Prime Minister Winston Churchill to announce that the British Expeditionary Force had been successfully evacuated from the port of Dunkirk in France, and to lay out Great Britain's hopes for the coming conflict—"victory at all costs."

As Churchill spoke, the Net Force Explorers scanned a map of Europe. Most of the continent had fallen to the might of the German Army. The escaping British soldiers would have been captured or killed by the Germans if they had spent even another day in France. As it was, only the valiant efforts of the Royal Air Force had kept the German Luftwaffe from bombing or strafing the rescue operation into a disastrous end. Over two hundred thousand British soldiers and over a hundred thousand Allied soldiers had been saved, and only two thousand men lost in the process.

It was one of the turning points of the war. Had the rescue at Dunkirk failed, Germany would almost certainly have been victorious in World War II. As it was, France surrendered to Germany on June 16th of 1940.

The images jumped again as the Net Force Explorers found themselves in a meeting of the British high command; then another jump took them among the German troops massing on the French coast, where assault boats were poised for an invasion of England. At last they were in the air once more, in the cockpit of a German bomber, as the Luftwaffe made daily attacks on British military installations from bases in France. The Battle of Britain had begun.

As they rode virtual Nazi bombers across the English Channel and over British soil, the Net Force Explorers heard a translation of Hermann Göring's speech to the German people, promising that his Luftwaffe would conquer the British people from the air.

Then the scene shifted again, and the Net Force Explorers

watched as British pilots took off in Spitfires and Hurricane fighters. From the virtual skies, swarms of German fighters and bombers rained death on England. The nation's only line of defense against the Nazi aggressors was the outnumbered and outgunned pilots of the Royal Air Force.

The Net Force Explorers found themselves at another Nazi rally, where they again heard Hermann Göring, this time wearing a sky-blue uniform festooned with medals, promise that no British bombs would fall on Berlin. Then they jumped into the cockpit of a British bomber on a daring nighttime raid on the German capital, the one that dropped the first bombs on Berlin.

Finally, the Net Force Explorers were in a meeting of the German high command, where Hitler himself ordered the bombing of London in retaliation for the attack on Berlin. The TeacherNet program concluded with waves of German fighters and bombers filling the morning sky as they headed for London.

After the rapid-fire program ended, the class broke for lunch and a chance to absorb what they'd learned. As the Net Force Explorers were sitting around the cafeteria, Andy Moore appeared, his face pale.

"I just read the roster for this afternoon," he said.

"And?" David Gray asked.

"We're going up against Dieter Rosengarten and the young Berliners again."

Everyone stopped eating and turned to Andy.

"Are you sure?" Matt Hunter asked. Andy nodded.

"The roster says that we're joining with a group of Brits from a school in London's East End, and going up against Dieter and Masahara Ito and the Japanese."

"The Japanese, too," Megan said, then moaned.

David looked at her. "What do you care?" he asked. "I bet those Japanese students are *afraid* of you. You're our team's *kamikaze*!"

Everyone laughed at that.

"These guys are only human," Matt said finally. "We can hold our own against them. We have to."

When they met back at class again that afternoon, the Net Force Explorers were sent into a veeyar simulation of a Royal

Air Force base outside London in the spring of 1940, where the British students were waiting to greet them.

When they entered veeyar, the Net Force Explorers found themselves standing in front of an old English cottage in a rural part of Britain. A flagpole with the familiar "Union Jack" flapping in the breeze towered over the small stone structure.

A wide farmer's field had been cleared and paved over, and in the distance there were lines of large, conical dun-colored tents where the men slept. Several hangars, a barn, and other rickety wooden structures housed single-engine propeller aircraft with the distinctive "bull's-eye" British tri-color markings on their wings and fuselage.

Several primitive tank trucks were scattered around the air field, holding fuel—*petrol*, as the British called it—for the airplanes. A bunch of airmen were pushing the planes out of the buildings, fueling them, and loading long belts of ammunition into the wing guns. They also performed other routine maintenance chores.

In the far distance, past a copse of tall trees, Matt could see a line of four delicate electronic towers. They were the radar stations, which would alert the British when the Germans were coming. Matt recalled what he'd learned in class that morning.

The British had invented radar in the late 1930's, and that technological achievement had probably saved them, and the world, from Nazi domination in the middle of the last century.

While young men in the prime of their lives threw their aircraft against the Germans in the skies, middle-aged British men, and young women of the RAF, monitored the primitive radar screens on the ground, searching for Heinkel He-111 bombers and Junkers Ju-87 Stukas. And their Messerschmitt Me-109 fighter escorts.

In the end, it was the radar, as much as the courage of the British airmen, that saved England from conquest. It was a reminder of just how important technological superiority really was in the modern world.

Matt scanned the peaceful scene before him. It was a bright, sunny spring morning and the air was fresh with the smell of new life. Hardly the setting for total war, Matt thought.

Mark Gridley tapped him on the shoulder and pointed to the cottage. Matt turned. Then he heard it too.

Singing.

Matt smiled at his wingman. "Let's go see who's having all the fun," he said. The rest of the Net Force Explorers followed.

When Matt pushed open the cottage door, a wave of sound almost blasted him backward. The Brits were singing an old World War II song called "Lily Marlane." As Matt strained to make out the words, he concluded that the song was about a woman waiting under a streetlight for the man of her dreams to come along . . . or something like that.

Suddenly, the Brits noticed the newcomers, and the singing died away. One of the British students rose and approached the Net Force Explorers. He had a severe haircut and an earring in one ear. There was a tattoo above his eye, a stylized picture of a lion roaring.

He was not what Matt was expecting.

The tattooed youth approached, and stuck out his hand to Matt.

"Pinky Brighton," he said by way of introduction. "You must be Matt 'unter, of Net Force."

Matt nodded, straining to understand the youth, whose Cockney accent was very thick, and who tended to drop the "H" off words beginning with that letter.

"I'm Matt Hunter," he said, shaking the youth's hand.

Pinky smiled brightly. "This 'ere's me wingman, Sadjit," Pinky said, putting his arm over the shoulder of a small youth of Indian descent.

"Come on in an' join the jollies," Pinky Brighton said, pointing to his mates.

The Net Force Explorers, grinning, mingled with the British youths. There was food on the table, a breakfast of tea and scones.

Matt thought about his father at that moment. *Remember, son,* his father would always say. *You can eat in veeyar, but it doesn't stick.* It was his way of reminding Matt that virtual reality was not *reality.*

The simulated ready room was very realistic, however. There were posters on the wall, many of them displaying the

"V for Victory" sign that was used to inspire the British in those dark days when they faced the Nazis alone.

There was another poster of a pretty woman named Vera Lynne. A British poster girl, Matt assumed.

"Just follow our lead, mate," Pinky Brighton said cheerily. "It's payback time for those Krauts." The other Brits loudly agreed with their leader, and they began to brag about what they were going to do to the Germans.

For a moment, Matt thought that these young British students were still fighting the Second World War in their minds. But as he listened to the drift of the conversation, he realized that the "payback" the Brits were referring to concerned last year's World Cup soccer match, where the British team was defeated by Germany.

Matt looked around, watching the Net Force Explorers interact with the Brits. Andy Moore was having fun. He really connected with these self-styled "soccer hooligans." Megan was speaking with a delicate young woman with an aristocratic bearing. She sat away from the rest of her team, enjoying their antics but seldom joining in.

Matt, meanwhile, was being bombarded by chatter from Pinky Brighton, who asked questions but seldom gave Matt the opportunity to answer.

"Feeling out of place a bit, eh?" Pinky asked during one typical exchange. Before Matt could reply, the Brit went on. "We'll just think of you Yanks as well-behaved Aussies!" he said.

"Or rambunctious Canadians," one of the other British youths said. Pinky nodded.

"You speak our language, mate," Pinky said. "That makes you one o' us."

Suddenly, the low moan of a siren began to wail, increasing in intensity as it went on and on.

"SCRAMBLE!" Pinky Brighton yelled, racing out of the cottage with the rest of the Brits in tow. Matt and the Net Force Explorers followed them, and together they all ran across the field, toward a line of waiting fighters—their engines already idling, filling the air with the smell of burning oil.

Matt hopped into the cockpit of his designated Spitfire, and an airman helped him strap in and don his canvas oxygen mask. He turned and saw Mark Gridley sitting in the aircraft to his right. He gave his wingman a thumbs-up.

Minutes later, the mock-RAF squadron took to the skies.

As they reached their patrol area, the combined squadrons looked around. Far below, the white chalk cliffs of Dover gleamed in the sun as the waves of the English Channel crashed against them. The sky was blue, the clouds drifting gently across it were puffy and white, and the Channel's waters were clear and sparkling.

"There they are," Pinky Brighton said over the radio.

Matt peered through the cockpit, straining to see the enemy. Suddenly, there they were, a swarm of twin-engine Heinkel He-111 bombers spread across the sky in tight formation.

As the Spitfires approached the enemy, Matt could make out more details. The German bombers were unique-looking airplanes. They had a long, rounded fuselage with a conical glass nose. The entire glass-walled front end of the aircraft served as the cockpit. There was a top gunner and a belly gunner on the bottom of the Heinkel's fuselage, to ward off attacks from those directions. The wings on the bombers were broad and rounded at the tips, and Matt could see the black crosses on the wings, and the swastika painted on their tails.

"In we go," Pinky said, suddenly not so jovial. "Watch for enemy fighters."

"Roger," Matt said. "Okay, guys," he said to his team. "Keep your eyes open."

"And good luck and good 'unting to us all." Pinky veered off after a target.

"I'm going for the bomber on the right," Matt said.

But Mark Gridley's reply was frantic.

"Watch your six!" Matt's wingman said, warning him that an enemy plane was coming up on his tail.

"We've got German fighters diving at us," David Gray said grimly. "Stay frosty!"

David barely finished his warning as bullets streamed out of the sky. One or two shells struck Matt's wing, and he jinked out of the way as a sky-blue single-engine Messerschmitt flashed past his cockpit.

"I'm on him," Mark said calmly. "You stick to the bombers."

Before Matt could reply, a Heinkel loomed ahead of him. Matt lined up his Spitfire on the bomber's tail and depressed the trigger. Though he was sure he hit the German plane, there was no visible damage as his Spitfire raced past the much slower German bomber.

"I'm hit!" Matt heard Megan O'Malley cry. He twisted in his seat, searching for his fellow Net Force Explorer. Then he saw her Spitfire spinning into the Channel, smoke and flames trailing behind. One of the Messerschmitt fighters had managed to hit her fuel tank.

"Good luck, Net Force Explorers," Megan said calmly as her aircraft spun out of control and struck the water with a huge splash.

Megan was gone.

Matt flipped his plane over and turned back toward the bombers, which were the real target of this exercise.

Seconds later, the Spitfires tore through the bombers, scattering the German formation on the first pass.

Pinky Brighton scored a kill almost immediately. His wing guns chattered and a Heinkel's right engine exploded, its propeller spinning down into the Channel. The bomber followed, plunging out of the blue sky in a long, grotesquely graceful vertical arc.

Matt selected a target, with Mark Gridley tight on his wing. Matt lined up behind a fleeing German bomber. He was surprised when tracers ripped past his wing. He'd forgotten about the rear gunner in the glass bubble on top of the Heinkel's fuselage.

Diving below the German gunner's bullets, Matt clutched the stick with a white-knuckled fist; then he depressed the trigger. His wing-mounted machine guns shook the whole Spitfire as the lead shells streaked toward their target. Bullets danced along the Heinkel's left wing. Matt tapped the joystick to the right, moving the stream of lead emerging from his guns.

His next burst ravaged the Heinkel's fuselage, and the plane broke up. To Matt's shock and surprise, a German—one of the virtual constructs, he hoped—tried to bail out. He was struck by some debris from his own stricken plane, and his body dropped limply through the clouds.

The parachute never deployed.

Again, Matt recalled something he'd learned in the TeacherNet that morning. "The British boys had to shoot the German boys down at a ratio of two to one just to maintain parity." He stole a glance at the earth below, and discovered that they were flying over British soil again.

He hadn't even noticed when they'd made landfall.

Matt saw several of the Brits engaging the German fighters, and Pinky Brighton's plane was drilling holes into a Messerschmitt, which plunged, burning, out of the sky. This time the pilot managed to bail out, and his parachute drifted lazily down toward a farmer's plowed field far below.

Matt could also hear the radio chatter from David Gray and Andy Moore. From the sound of things, they were holding their own, and maybe doing even better than that.

"Got him!" David said. Out of the corner of his eye, Matt saw a Messerschmitt explode in midair. Its orange fireball lit up the sky.

Andy, glued to David's wing, opened up too. He dispatched another German fighter in less than three seconds.

It appeared that the Net Force Explorers were doing a lot better in the area of air combat, and Matt felt a rush of pride.

Suddenly, Mark Gridley slid up to Matt's right wing once again. Matt turned and gave his wingman another thumbs-up.

"How did you do, Squirt?" Matt asked.

"Call me Squirt no more," Mark said triumphantly. "I downed a German bomber, and my first Messerschmitt."

"Good shooting," Matt said.

"I'm beginning to *like* it," Mark said. "In fact, I could do this all day!"

"Good," Matt said, his eyes narrowing. "Then you'll be happy to know that we have more company coming our way."

Mark peered through his cockpit in time to see a line of five Messerschmitt Me-109's streaking out of the sun and right for them at top speed.

As Dr. Lanier congratulated the Net Force Explorers on their best performance in the flight simulators yet, the team looked as if they had lost the war.

Their expressions were grim as Dr. Lanier read them their tally. But if the professor noticed their strange reaction, he said nothing, which was a relief for Matt. He couldn't explain to his teacher what was wrong anyway.

There was no doubt that the Net Force Explorers had done well. Matt, Mark, and David had survived the simulation to the very end. Andy would have survived too if it wasn't for his obsession with Dieter Rosengarten.

Andy had spotted the German's fighter near the end of the competition and, ignoring David Gray's warning, he went after "Baron von Dieter."

And was promptly shot down.

But even that blow to Andy's fragile ego paled when Matt, Mark, and David snapped back to real-time with the bad news. They had seen no sign of Julio Cortez, or his familiar orange fighter plane. The three of them had flown in circles over Great Britain, scanning the skies in search of their friend, until the simulation ended and they were thrust back to reality.

It appeared that Julio was gone, almost as if he had never been there at all.

9

The Net Force Explorers headed home as soon as the seminar ended on Monday afternoon. Matt had called a meeting for after dinner to give them time to think about the problem, and everyone was planning to attend. The autobus was crowded, so they didn't talk about Julio.

As the team rode back to the burbs, Matt hardly spoke to the rest of them at all. The other Net Force Explorers, sensing his distress, gave him space. For a while, they talked among themselves about nothing in particular. But soon, everyone sank into a despondent silence.

Matt stared unseeing as the neighborhoods flashed by outside the window. He was lost in his own thoughts, torn by doubt, and by fear. Fear for his friend, and for his own sanity.

I know I saw Julio in the simulator, he thought. *So why wasn't he there today? Those first two times couldn't all just be the result of my imagination—heightened by the chaotic patterns of a Rift.*

He reminded himself that Mark Gridley had seen the same thing as he did. The first time anyway.

But Matt also recalled that he was on his own the second time Julio appeared, in the Battle of Midway simulation.

I know I didn't imagine it, he thought. Then he remembered the doctored news broadcast of Julio and his family.

At that moment he realized that the other Net Force Explorers had been acting on his claims as if they were already proven for days. And in a way, they had been—would Corteguay have dummied up that news broadcast if Julio and his family were free and happy? But the Net Force Explorers had acted on his mere word that Julio was in trouble, long before they'd even seen that doctored broadcast.

The Net Force Explorers trust me. They took my word that something was wrong, and acted on it, he realized. *They may question what I say at first, we may argue a bit, but in the final analysis, my friends trust me.*

With that realization, Matt felt better. And the important thing now was not to give up. Matt knew he would think of something, and if *he* didn't, then one of the other Net Force Explorers would.

He trusted them too.

Though Matt felt better, the rest of the team was feeling pretty bad. Their mood had not improved by the time they hooked up to their computers that evening and met at the virtual Net Force Explorers' Lounge. The room they were in this time was a huge space filled with every gadget, gizmo, and gimmick that the student programmers in the Net Force Explorers could think of, from walls that changed form and color with each passing second to shimmering fountains whose waters wove in and among the seats without ever seeming to touch their occupants or interfere with what anybody wanted to watch.

Sights, sounds, and scents merged to create a wonderful environment to meet in or just think. It was a cheerful, busy place, but today it wasn't enough to snap the Net Force Explorers out of their gloom.

''What next?'' Megan asked after Matt called the meeting to order.

The others looked at Matt Hunter expectantly, waiting for him to decide their next course of action.

Matt returned their stare. ''I say we keep trying to contact Julio, but I'm also willing to listen to anybody's suggestion for our next move.''

''I still think we should go public,'' Andy Moore said once again. The others objected, but not so vehemently this time.

Matt worried that they would soon disobey Jay Gridley's instructions not to tell anyone else about this while Net Force investigated on its own.

Even Matt himself was having doubts. Though he kept them to himself, he couldn't help but feel that so far the State Department and the government of Corteguay were giving everyone the runaround. Their delaying tactics were costing valuable time, time in which anything could be happening to Julio and his family. Maybe the Net Force Explorers *should* go public themselves, or at least leak the story to the press or something.

David Gray felt the same way, and he said so.

"Why don't we alert the media?" David said. "Surely someone will listen to us. Corteguay's in the news; there's always someone looking for a story."

"There are risks in going public," Matt warned. "It might force the Corteguan government into doing something really bad, like making Julio and his family disappear to hide the truth."

"Haven't they done that already?" Megan asked.

"But maybe not permanently—at least not yet," Matt said. That gave them all room for pause.

The Net Force Explorers were still debating various courses of action when they were interrupted by a familiar voice.

"Permission to join the meeting?" Jay Gridley asked, to everyone's astonishment. The head of Net Force almost never came down to this level of the Net, let alone to the Net Force Explorers' Lounge. Though his tone and demeanor indicated that this was a social call, Matt couldn't help feeling that it was a surprise inspection by his commanding officer.

"Permission granted, sir," Matt said.

"With pleasure," Megan O'Malley seconded.

The head of Net Force sat down, and placed a two-inch datascript icon on the table in front of him. Everyone recognized the logo on the 'script. It was today's *Washington Times*.

"I was expecting you to report to me as soon as you got back," Mr. Gridley said.

Matt frowned. "The problem is that we don't *have* anything to report." They told him about Julio failing to appear in today's simulator.

"Don't give up," Mr. Gridley said. "There could be a lot of reasons for that." He tapped the datascript with his index finger. "Like this, for instance."

He placed the datascript into the computer and the front spread of the newssheet was displayed, glittering in midair, where everybody could see it. Gridley pointed at one of the lead stories.

The headline read: "FIND THE MISSING CANDIDATE." The subhead asked, "How Can Ramon Cortez Win Corteguay's Election Without Campaigning?"

The story was written by someone named Carrie Page.

"Is this good or bad?" Matt asked.

Jay Gridley thought about it for a minute before he replied.

"It puts pressure on Corteguay's regime," he said. "No doubt about *that*. But the pressure could have positive or negative results. It's up to the Corteguans. The ball is in their court."

"I'll bet it puts pressure on the State Department, too," Megan said.

Gridley nodded and smiled conspiratorially.

"Apparently so," he said. "I've been in contact with Ms. Page of the *Times,* and she thinks she may have forced the State Department's hand."

"In what way?" David Gray asked.

"She has been requesting a travel visa to enter Corteguay for months," he told them. "So far, her requests have been denied. But now she thinks that State will have to arrange a video conference in the next few days. Other members of the media are becoming interested, and Ms. Page is very persistent. To satisfy her, and several other news organizations that have been asking questions, State has opened some diplomatic channels. We should see some results in a few hours."

"Video conferences can be faked," Megan said. "Remember the Zaibatsu coup in Japan. That holoform Emperor fooled everyone, for a while at least."

"Yeah," Mark Gridley said. "But that was the Japanese. They have some of the best virtual equipment in the world. We're talking about Corteguay now. How can *they* fool *us*?"

"Don't be too quick to dismiss their veeyar capabilities,"

his father said. "They've had help in the past. From Cuba Libre, and from the Asian Freebooters."

Matt had heard of both terrorist groups. Cuba Libre was a cadre of true believers, who still fought for Fidel Castro's cause, left over from the days when Castro and his communists were ousted and sent into exile in Iran.

The Freebooters were even tougher. They had a new and original political agenda. The Freebooters believed that the achievement of any single individual was automatically the property of everyone—hence all copyrights and trade treaties were invalid and unjust.

Naturally, the Freebooters' philosophy caused them to pirate every invention they could get their hands on. That kind of pirating was theft, pure and simple—computer crime's newest twist.

"Well," Matt asked, "if the Corteguans *can* trick us, then what's to stop them from doing it?"

Jay Gridley looked right at him. "You," he said.

An hour after the Net Force Explorer meeting broke up, Matt Hunter, who was ordered by Jay Gridley to stick around after the meeting, was summoned to the office of Net Force's head—in reality. A short trip on the autobus later, he sat in front of Jay Gridley.

"Matt," Gridley said, "I'd like you to meet Mr. Walter Paulson, of the State Department."

Matt took a look at the man, shook his hand, and wondered if he was touching a snake. He had inherited his father's abhorrence of Ivy League types, and Paulson was a prime example of the breed, right down to the school tie and the tweed blazer with leather patches on the elbows.

"The State Department needs your help, Mr. Hunter," Paulson said after they sat down. "I hope you will not refuse us."

"What can I do for you?" Matt asked.

"Tomorrow evening, we have arranged a video conference with some members of the Cortez family," he said. Matt's heart leaped, but he remained outwardly calm.

"Ramon Cortez will speak with some members of the national press," Paulson continued. "Due to the concerns expressed by Mr. Gridley here, we have also arranged a second video conference following the first. A conference with your friend, Julio Cortez.''

"And you want me to attend," Matt said.

Walter Paulson nodded. ''In the interest of your own peace of mind,'' he said.

"What about my friends?'' Matt asked. ''Will they be allowed to attend, too?''

Paulson nodded. ''Just as long as their questions are brief. We'll only have a few minutes.''

"That's fine,'' Matt said.

"The State Department makes only one more request,'' Paulson said. Matt and Jay Gridley waited for the other shoe to drop.

"We know that Ms. Carrie Page, a reporter for the *Washington Times,* would like to be allowed to attend your conference. She may want to interview you and the other Net Force Explorers afterwards.''

Inwardly, Matt breathed a huge sigh of relief.

"That would be fine, Mr. Paulson,'' he said. Then Walter Paulson rose, signaling the end of the meeting.

"I'll see you tomorrow then,'' he said. ''Seven o'clock. The conference will take place right here at Net Force. I look forward to seeing everyone, and to putting this matter to rest once and for all. . . .''

Twelve hours later, the Net Force Explorers were gathered outside one of Net Force headquarters' main conference rooms. As they loitered near the closed doors, Matt wondered what was going on inside.

According to Jay Gridley, who had stopped to speak to them before going in, what was taking place now was the first video conference with Ramon Cortez, Julio's father. At that closed session, Ramon Cortez would be interviewed by several members of the press, who would then pool their stories with other news agencies.

The presidential candidate would also be grilled by Lettie Hanratty, the former U.S. ambassador to Corteguay.

None of the Net Force Explorers were permitted to attend that formal conference. Their less formal talk with Julio was scheduled for after the main event, whenever that would be.

Already, the first conference had gone over the allotted time, and the Net Force Explorers could do nothing more than wait for their turn. Their impatience began to show. Matt, especially, was growing anxious. The longer he waited, the more he worried.

Matt wondered if he had the brains to outsmart a hostile government. So much was riding on his actions today—including Julio's life. Was he going to be the victim of a government cover-up? Or was he really going to be speaking with his best friend?

I hope so, Matt thought with a sigh. But he still had nagging doubts that just wouldn't go away.

Across the hall, Megan sat with David Gray. The two of them seemed composed, compared to Matt. *Well, all they have to do is listen,* he thought enviously. *They didn't know Julio as well as I did.*

Then Matt turned to the youngest member of the group.

There was tension on Mark Gridley's young face too. The thirteen-year-old had known Julio well, though not as well as Matt. Matt Hunter hoped that he could trust the Squirt to smell out any deceptions he missed.

At that moment, the double doors swung open and a group of reporters filed out of the conference room, talking furiously. The reporters were already starting to think through their stories for the various media.

Walter Paulson also emerged from the conference room with an assistant in tow. He walked right past Matt, but didn't even acknowledge him. Instead, he concentrated on speaking with the reporters, trying to gauge the drift of the stories they would soon file.

From what Matt could hear, the State Department policy wonk was working on spin control, not on getting at the truth. Matt tuned the man's words out. He preferred to make his own decision, thank you very much.

Jay Gridley emerged next. The head of Net Force was speaking with a tall, striking, reed-thin woman with craggy features, a shock of wild gray hair, and intelligent eyes. Matt recognized her instantly. Lettie Hanratty, the former ambassador to Corteguay.

The woman was smiling as she spoke, and Matt wondered

if that meant she was satisfied by the conference.

Jay Gridley spotted the Net Force Explorers out of the corner of his eye, but he could not politely break away from Ms. Hanratty, who was speaking intently about some topic or other.

Suddenly, a beautiful young woman with short red hair burst out of the crowd of reporters. She was wearing a skin-tight black jumpsuit, and high-heeled boots in a fashionable faux-animal-skin print, and right now she was pushing through the crowd toward Matt. She stopped right in front of him.

"You must be Matt Hunter of the Net Force Explorers," she said, her voice sweet and surprisingly girlish. "My name is Carrie Page. I'm a reporter for the *Washington Times*."

She thrust out her hand, and Matt shook it. Her grip was firm, yet still feminine. Matt was impressed by the combination. The woman's striking green eyes stared at Matt intensely, as if she were trying to memorize every detail of his appearance for memory access later. Matt judged her to be in her early twenties—not that much older than he was, Matt realized.

After a moment her intense gaze made him uncomfortable, and Matt hoped he didn't blush. Carrie Page pushed some hair away from her forehead and raised her computer.

"So, how long have you known Julio Cortez?" she asked, getting down to business. When he answered, Matt knew that the datapad she carried was recording every thing he was saying.

She sure is thorough, Matt marveled. He liked that in a woman. . . .

Fifteen minutes later, Walter Paulson led the Net Force Explorers, Jay Gridley, and Carrie Page back into the video conference room. Due to the unusual rules that governed press contacts in Corteguay, they wouldn't be using virtual technology for this interview. Two-dee technology was all that was allowed. As a result, they were treated to the unusual sight of a large flat-screen dominating the far wall, with all the chairs in the room lined up facing it.

A technician sat at the control board, waiting for his cue to reestablish communication with Corteguay.

Before that occurred, Walter Paulson went to the front of the room and addressed them briefly.

"This call will only last about five minutes," he said. "Mateo Cortez only has access to the government video facility for a limited period of time, and the first conference took considerably longer than Mateo had budgeted for."

Matt listened calmly, but inside he was in turmoil. Mark Gridley sat on his right, and Carrie Page on his left. As Paulson spoke, the journalist ignored the bureaucrat and continuously made notes on her computer's datapad. Matt's close proximity to this lovely woman increased his discomfort, but he tried to tough it out as best he could.

Finally, Paulson finished his speech, and nodded toward the technician. The man at the control board, in obvious defiance of the State Department wonk, turned and faced his own boss.

Jay Gridley nodded too, and the technician went to work.

A moment later, the flat-screen came to life in a swirl of colors. Then, quicker than anyone expected, the smiling face of Julio Cortez appeared on the screen.

The image was fairly clear, but disconcerting in appearance to Matt and his friends, who'd grown up in the age of holographic, three-dimensional broadcasts. The audio was crystal clear, however, and the group could even hear the sounds of people speaking in the background, out of camera range.

Julio was wearing a blue silk shirt under his leather flight jacket. When the connection was completed, Julio focused on Matt, who was sitting in the front row.

"Matt, *mi hombre*," Julio said with a twinkle of his eye. "How you doin'?"

Before Matt could reply, Julio's gaze shifted.

"It's the Squirt!" Julio said, pointing at Mark Gridley. "I see you haven't grown much. My sister Juanita could still take you, kid!"

Mark smiled, but said nothing. As per Walter Paulson's instructions, he waited his turn.

"I'm doing just fine, Julio," Matt finally said guardedly. "How about you? How are things in Corteguay?"

"This place is really something," Julio continued. "There's good and there's bad. Like anywhere else, I guess."

Out of the corner of his eyes, Matt noticed Mark Gridley

staring at the screen. The Squirt was still smiling, though, apparently convinced that they were really talking to Julio Cortez.

"You should see the computers they got here, man," Julio continued on, rolling his eyes as he spoke. "Yesterday I saw a Macintosh, with one of those old-fashioned mouse things on it. Some guy was working with that antique, can you believe it? The Mac *wasn't* in a museum. It was still being used!"

Matt heard some of the Net Force Explorers chuckle.

"I even saw an old word processor," Julio continued. "I said to the guy running it, 'Hey, man, why don't you get a typewriter?' Real sarcastic, you know? He said, seriously, that he had one in the other room, but he just wasn't using it today!"

The image of Julio on the screen shook his head in amazement, and Matt recognized the gesture as pure Julio.

"But it's not all bad," Julio went on. "The girls here are very impressive. And 'cause my dad's running for president, I'm being treated like a pop star!"

Then Julio's eyes narrowed, and he focused on Carrie Page.

"I see you've been real busy too, Matt," Julio said with a trace of envy. "Introduce me to the lady beside you."

Matt, almost blushing, introduced Julio to Ms. Page. She nodded a greeting, but did not speak, leaving the valuable conference time to Matt and the Net Force Explorers, as the State Department representative had requested.

"We really miss you, Julio," Matt said.

"I miss you guys too," Julio said. "But as soon as my dad is elected president, we'll get some veeyar technology here in Adello and we can all play together again."

"So you don't have much opportunity to use veeyar?" Megan O'Malley asked from the second row.

Julio smiled. "Hey, Megan," he said. "I didn't see you back there."

"Yeah," Mark Gridley chimed in. "How do you live without veeyar?"

Julio shook his head. "It's tough, I'll tell you. I really miss the flight simulators!"

"You're missing the Century of Military Aviation competitions," Mark continued. "We could really use you in there."

"I'll bet you're all doing just fine without me," Julio said humbly. "Even you, Squirt!"

Mark smiled. "I shot down a Messerschmitt yesterday," he said proudly.

"Good for you!" Julio said enthusiastically.

"We have to fight screaming out your call sign, Julio," Matt said in a neutral voice. "Until you moved, when we got into real trouble, we always knew who to call."

"Don't worry," Julio said, turning his back to the video-camera so that the Net Force Explorers could read the glow-script on his jacket. "The Ace of Aces will soon fly again!"

At that moment, Matt's heart went cold. He felt Mark stiffen at his side. But the Squirt held on to his control.

Matt did too, though it was hard.

Suddenly, Carrie Page leaned forward in her chair.

"Is that your call sign?" she asked evenly. "Ace of Aces?" The image on the screen nodded. "That's me!" it said.

To Matt, the image was just an *it* now—he and the rest of the Net Force Explorers knew that the image they were watching was a fake.

The image on the screen was not their friend.

Julio's call sign was *Jefe,* not Ace of Aces. Whoever was running the show had made a natural enough error, considering the logo emblazoned on Julio's jacket.

But whoever they were speaking to, it was definitely not their friend Julio Cortez.

10

Mateo Cortez was summoned to the complex in the jungle almost as soon as the farce that was the video conference with the North American press was completed. The summons was inconvenient. Mateo had too much to do in Adello to waste hours making the trip, and he did not understand why his master wished to see him again so soon.

But Mateo Cortez had been conditioned not to ask questions, simply to obey. So when he was called, Mateo came.

Once again, as a precaution, Mateo took the ancient, battered Hummer instead of a more modern, and more comfortable, military vehicle. And this time he drove himself. Already he felt that too many soldiers in the capital knew about this place. Mateo thought it was unwise to call attention to the installation with too much activity.

There were spies everywhere, and the Yanqui had very effective satellite capabilities. But of course, to use them, the Norteamericanos had to have a good idea of what they were looking for.

Mateo doubted they had a clue.

So, after taking all of these precautions, it came as a shock when Mateo rounded the corner on the rutted jungle road and saw a large, modern transport truck parked in front of the concrete bunker. And he was doubly surprised when he saw a group of technicians uncrating some state-of-the-art computers and loading them into the wide-open freight elevator.

Most of the men in white lab coats were Asian, Mateo noted. The Asian Freebooters were increasing their influence in Corteguay every day. Soon they would be almost as troubling as the Americans, Mateo realized.

As he approached the gate, the soldiers—Cuban exiles, he'd been told once—who guarded this place waved Mateo through without checking his identity, or even making sure that his vehicle held no foreign commandos hiding in its backseat or in the trunk.

Sloppy, Mateo thought, shaking his head in disgust. *Damn sloppy . . .*

The guards, he noticed, appeared harried and put upon—which suggested to Mateo that this truck was not the first to arrive in the past few days. That thought alarmed him. Mateo cursed when he parked his Hummer and saw the tracks of several trucks in the crushed grass.

But at least the Cuban who admitted him into the bunker itself was thorough in his search and identity check, and Mateo still had to wait for the retinal scan before he could board the elevator and descend into the pit.

When the elevator doors slid open deep underground, Mateo had yet another surprise in store for him. The once-spacious tunnel, hollowed out by pumping an underground river dry, was now crowded with shining new computers wired into a network.

The seven tables, with their wired prisoners, were still in place, but a totally new control station had been assembled in the opposite corner of the cave.

There was no sign of the slovenly woman who cared for the prisoners, but Mateo noticed that the hostages had been cleaned and given fresh, new sheets and blankets. Then Mateo saw two men loitering near the new control center. Curious, Mateo approached them.

One man Mateo recognized immediately. His name was Sato, and his tattoos—and a missing little finger on his left hand—marked the Japanese man as Yakuza. According to the dossier Mateo had read, Sato was a gangster from Osaka, a hired killer who murdered his victims over the Net, impossible as that seemed.

At least that was the rumor.

The other man was probably a Cuban, judging by his clothing, though Mateo didn't recognize him. The man's features were slack as he leaned against a mainframe, laconically talking to Sato. The man's head turned, and Mateo noticed then that the Cuban was a Drex-Dream addict, plugged into an injection system that delivered the drug directly to his cerebral cortex. The metal and Lexan reservoir attached to his skull gleamed in the artificial light.

Mateo shuddered.

At one point early in the century, as more and more of the business and pleasure of the world was conducted on the Net, a few medical researchers had seen a huge opportunity for profit. Computers thought faster than men, and by 2010 the Net was limited only by its weakest link—the humans who used it. The researchers thought that if they could find and patent a drug that would speed up mental activity without physical side effects, they could become richer than Bill Gates had become in the previous century. Businessmen, traders, professional and amateur game players—anybody who used the Net on a regular basis—would pay any amount of money for a drug that gave them an edge over the competition.

Drex-Dream had been the result of the researchers' work. Unlike most drugs that had an effect on the ability of the brain to process information, Drex-Dream radically improved neural transmission speeds, comprehension, ability to focus, and memory, all without affecting heart rate or blood pressure or demonstrating any of the other common negative side effects of such drugs.

An early, small-scale human trial had looked promising. Then the trial ended. Two of the volunteer subjects of the test were killed trying to break into the lab for more of the drug. Three more went mad. Every person that participated in the trial suffered from some level of addiction. Most were unable to function in the world after being denied a continued supply of Drex-Dream. Because of this, the FDA refused to approve the drug, and the researchers went on to other things. But one of Drex-Dream's marketers decided that his future was made. He and the drug went underground.

The Drex-Dream trial had been at controlled, clinical dosages. When Drex-Dream was put out on the street by a few select illegal drug dealers, those limits no longer applied. Those who used Drex-Dream in street dosages maintained that the high was indescribable. They were also hopelessly addicted after a single dose.

Most Drex-Dream addicts died quickly as a result of their addiction. While taking the drug, the users wouldn't stop to eat, drink, or sleep. They starved or died of thirst, often while within reach of the very things that would save them.

Mateo noticed that this man had a timer on his injector, a digital clock with red flashing numbers that automatically distributed the drug in specified quantities at given times. That was one way that Drex-Dream addicts controlled their addictions, but it was only a temporary fix. At some point, probably in the not too distant future, the Cuban would succumb to temptation and unleash the drug continuously. While he was under the influence, he would be inhumanly fast on the Net, inhumanly swift in thought and reaction time. And then, a few weeks later, he would die from self-induced dehydration or starvation.

"I see you have met our new allies," his master's voice said from behind him. Mateo turned.

His controller was smiling at him.

"How did the conference go?" his master asked.

"The holoform Ramon fooled everyone, even that woman Hanratty," Mateo said. "The holo of Julio . . . I am not so sure."

"You think those *boys* saw through our ruse?" the master asked incredulously. Mateo paused before answering.

"I . . . I feel that they still had doubts," he said. "But nothing concrete, and no proof. We were too thorough for that."

"I am not surprised," his master said. Mateo stared again at the two strangers, afraid to guess their function but too intimidated to ask. When Mateo faced his master again, the man was still smiling at Mateo. That made Mateo very nervous.

"I told you the last time you were here that I suspected that Julio had escaped," the man said. "Fortunately, the automatic security program overrode his mind. Unfortunately, the program could not tell me where he went or how he got out."

The master gazed at Mateo. "Where do you think your nephew fled, Mateo?" he asked.

The younger man blinked and shrugged. "I am not sure," Mateo said. "To the State Department computers possibly. The media. Perhaps even to Net Force or the FBI."

"I think he went to find those boys," the master said. "His friends in the Net Force Explorers."

"Then perhaps the conference was a mistake," Mateo said. "Perhaps these children are now suspicious."

"They were suspicious before this," the master said. "Your nephew Julio has communicated with them, I'm certain of it!"

Mateo faced the two strangers again.

The Japanese man continued to stare placidly into space, ignoring everything around him. The other man leaned on the cabinet and carefully contemplated something only he could see.

"Is that why these assassins are here?" Mateo asked.

The master reached up and patted Mateo on the shoulder, stroking him as if he were a particularly intelligent dog.

"As I promised you last time," the master said, pointing at the two men, "these men are here to deal with Julio's allies in the outside world." The master smiled again. It was the grin of a cruel predator. "Virtual assassins," he whispered softly. "The best our sponsors could buy."

The man hooked to the Drex-Dream injector suddenly moaned, then began to giggle like a madman.

For many hours after the conference, the Net Force Explorers remained in the Lounge, discussing their next move endlessly. Their attempts to tell the grown-ups that something was radically wrong had been rebuffed by everyone except Jay Gridley, who'd said he would check into it—but made no promises of further action. The State Department people had been especially dismissive. One even went so far as to accuse the Net Force Explorers of trying to capitalize on the media attention focused on Julio and his family. It was clear that they, and they alone, believed that their friend was in trouble. If something was going to be done about it, they were going to have to get undeniable proof of wrongdoing, and enough information to save Julio. But everybody had a different idea about the best way to get it.

As they argued, Megan O'Malley zoned out, lost in her own thoughts.

Where is Julio being held? How can he be freed? What will happen once the election in Corteguay is over? And will the end result be different if Ramon wins instead of losing?

These were only a few of the questions that whirled through Megan O'Malley's mind as she listened to the others talk.

Though the first few hours of their impromptu meeting were spent debating possible plans, the Net Force Explorers had yet to decide on any specific action to take.

Soon, as if they were attending Julio Cortez's wake, Matt and Mark started to talk about their friendship with Julio, and about the young Corteguan's love of flight simulators. Eventually, the conversation centered on last year's Century of Military Aviation competition, where Julio came in second. Megan learned only then that Julio was the sole Net Force Explorer to participate last year. Things were different this year, thanks to Julio's example. Matt wished he could have competed with his friend, but Matt's family had been traveling last summer, so he had been unable to join Julio in the competition.

Mark "the Squirt" Gridley would have participated too, but he'd been too young to compete until now.

"Was Dieter Rosengarten there last year?" Andy Moore asked.

"I don't think so," Matt said, shaking his head. "But there was this Russian guy named Sergei who cleaned everybody's clocks. He was almost as good as Pavel Ivanovich, who won!" Matt chuckled then. "Well, Sergei was good, but not as good as Julio," he remembered. "Near the end of the competition, in the Bosnia scenario, Julio ruined Sergei's perfect score by shooting him down. The only perfect score was Ivanovich's, so Julio cost Sergei a shot at the Ace of Aces trophy. Ivanovich came in first. Julio and Sergei were tied with one loss each, but since Julio'd taken Sergei out, Julio came in second, and Sergei came in third."

Megan smiled. "I'll bet Julio dug those Japanese a new hole at Pearl Harbor too," she said, joining in the conversation.

Matt shook his head.

"He didn't compete in the Pearl Harbor simulator last year," he told her. "He didn't participate in the Battle of Britain either."

Suddenly, something clicked in Megan's brain. She sat up quickly. "What simulators *did* he compete in last year?" she asked. "How many different sims did he try?"

Matt knew that look on Megan's face. She was on to something. Matt considered his answers carefully.

"He competed in five scenarios in the first round," he said. "The Red Baron first, followed by the Battle of Midway, the Bombing of Europe, the Bosnian Crisis of 2007, and the South African War in 2010."

"And *this* year Julio appeared in the Red Baron and the Battle of Midway. . . ." Megan thought aloud.

Matt's eyes got wide.

"And *not* Pearl Harbor or the Battle of Britain!" he said. "Do you think—"

"I think that Julio only shows up in simulators he's experienced before!" Megan said. "That's why we didn't see him the other day. He'd never experienced the Battle of Britain simulator before."

"That's it!" Mark Gridley said. "That has to be it. Think about it. You know how, when you first try a new veeyar program, it's like trying anything for the first time? You make mistakes, don't take advantage of all the breaks, sometimes you even get bounced out doing something stupid—so it always takes a while to get familiar with it?"

"But once you get the hang of it, it gets easier and easier, until it's second nature," David Gray said. "Julio's got so much to cope with already, he's avoiding adding that kind of stress to his problems. That's gotta be it. It's too much of a coincidence not to be."

Suddenly, Matt got a stricken look on his face. Megan noticed it right away.

"What's wrong?" she asked.

"We're not signed up for the Bombing of Europe," Matt said. "We're supposed to do MiG Alley, a Korean War simulation, next."

"What about the other two sims Julio did in the early

rounds?'' Andy asked. ''Bosnia and the South African War?''

Matt nodded. ''We're doing Bosnia again. And everybody has to do the South African War,'' he said. ''The South African War has all the most modern high-tech fighters, stuff like the Joint Strike Fighters.''

''Well, then, we've got to find a way to get into the Bombing of Europe simulator,'' Megan said.

But Matt shook his head.

''Can't be done,'' he said. ''The competition is fixed ahead of time. We *have* to do the Korean War sim, or we'll get disqualified—which means no more access to the simulators.'' Matt shrugged his shoulders. ''There are no substitutions, unless they're made by the Institute staff. It's not up to us.''

''But what if something bad were to happen?'' Mark asked with a devilish grin. ''Something so bad it messed that Korean War simulator up so that we can't use it.''

Andy Moore looked at the Squirt. ''Do you have the chips to try something like that?'' he asked.

''No,'' Mark said. ''I'm not stupid. And you heard what my dad said.''

Andy nodded.

''But I know someone who *does* have the chips necessary, and a whole lot more,'' Mark said. ''And if we ask her nicely enough, she just might do it.''

As Mark told Joanna Winthrop the Net Force Explorers' conclusions, he could tell she was listening to them as though their concerns were real ones. She even admitted that their reasoning was sound, given all the unknowns and variables involved in Julio's bizarre case.

When he and the Net Force Explorers had finished explaining their logic, it was Mark Gridley who dropped the other shoe, though in this case it was more like a bomb.

''We were wondering,'' he said in his most innocent and endearing voice, ''if we could maybe come up with a way to crash their Korean War simulator.''

''Yeah,'' Matt Hunter chimed in. ''Nothing too drastic. Just mess it up for a day or two . . .''

''That way they would probably have us compete in the Bombing of Europe simulation,'' David Gray added.

"And I'm sure we'll find Julio in there," Megan concluded. Joanna scanned their eager faces, and she clearly realized that she was outnumbered and outflanked.

"I don't like this," she said. "I don't like this one bit."

"Please," Mark cajoled. *"Pleasepleaseplease..."*

His pleading was so comical that it made Joanna Winthrop burst out laughing, as well as the other Net Force Explorers. His clown act was intentional. After she was overcome with mirth, Mark knew Joanna was easy prey.

"All right, all right, but I refuse to do any permanent damage," she agreed finally. "And you have to help!"

"Just name it," Matt said. "All of us will help."

"I only need one of you," Joanna said.

"Who do you want?" Mark asked, curious.

"You, Mark," Joanna answered. "I need you to give me everything you know about the system—and I want you to help me come up with a relatively harmless computer virus, something with a timer attached, so that things go back to normal after a specified time. If I'm going to crack that simulator, I want all the information I can get first, and I want to leave it intact after I'm done with it."

Mark Gridley gulped, but nodded.

Mark Gridley stopped talking, waiting expectantly for Joanna Winthrop's reaction. He'd just explained how he'd developed the virus, and what it would do to the flight simulators. Mark didn't tell her that he'd worked through the night creating the cyber-disease, and that it was the hardest job he'd ever tackled.

"I'd hate to have to go up against you in a cyber-war," Joanna said after a moment.

Her simple statement made Mark beam with pride. It was as close to offering a compliment as Joanna ever got, and Mark basked in her approval.

"So are you ready to put the virus into the system?" she asked.

Mark nodded.

She gave the computer a quiet vocal command. An icon appeared in the middle of the veeyar, the image of a huge hypodermic needle. As Mark and Joanna watched, the "needle" filled up with the virus program until the hypodermic turned red, indicating that all of the virus had been downloaded into the delivery system.

The word "ACTIVE" flashed before their eyes.

"Now we just have to crack the IEI's firewall," Joanna said. "I did a little work on that early this morning."

Mark realized she'd found a back door left behind by the system's original designer. She keyed in the names of the man's children and pets in a certain order—amazing what you could find out with a little research—and the defenses melted before their eyes. Almost immediately, the IEI's simulator control page opened up to them. Each simulation was a separate software program, something that made their next task a lot easier.

Fearing a trace on their activities, Joanna quickly loaded the Korean War simulation and opened it. Then she aimed the hypodermic needle icon into the heart of the flight simulator program.

"You're certain this won't do any real damage?" Joanna asked.

Mark shook his head. "It's a virus that will actually self-destruct in less than twenty-four hours," he said proudly. "I had my dad check the virus out and he approved it."

"Like the twenty-four-hour flu," Joanna said with a laugh. Mark nodded.

"Then let's fire away!" she said. Joanna Winthrop caught Mark's eye. "And don't try this at home again unless your dad is involved, okay?" she warned him.

The boy nodded. He remembered all too well the look on his father's face when he'd discovered Mark's recent activities.

She plunged the tip of the needle into the simulation, injecting the virus into the software, exited the program, and began scanning the simulation computer's directory.

"What are you doing, Joanna?" Mark asked.

"Just laying a few small traps. We wouldn't want them to be able to reload a working copy of this simulation from backup datascripts, would we?" And with a smile on her face, the sort of smile a cat who finds itself in an aviary might wear, she turned back to her work.

•   •   •

The next morning, as the Net Force Explorers arrived at the International Educational Institute's seminar room, a grim Dr. Lanier was there to greet them.

"I truly apologize, Net Force Explorers," he said with genuine regret. "But we've experienced another problem. This time in the Korean War simulator."

"Oh, no," Andy Moore said with amazingly sincere disappointment in his voice. "You mean we can't use it?"

Dr. Lanier nodded. "I'm afraid so," he said. "It has presented us with a real problem, one that we're working on solving. The manufacturer is going to download a new copy of the software tonight," the professor continued. "But I think I've come up with a solution that will suffice in the meantime."

Dr. Lanier pushed a button on the podium and the lights dimmed. A huge, panoramic hologram of a formation of four-engine bombers, with fighter escort in tow, filled the room above them.

"I think you'll like our substitute simulation," Dr. Lanier said hopefully.

"It's all about the daring daylight bombing raids over Nazi Germany. . . ."

"In 1943, the United States Eighth Air Force, based in England, began daring daylight heavy bombing raids over Germany." Dr. Lanier lectured off the cuff, and without the benefit of a TeacherNet.

Instead, harrowing images on the wall behind him came to dramatic life with black and white flatfilm of huge, four-engine, propeller-driven B-17 Flying Fortress bombers, literally hundreds of them, flying in formation over the European landscape.

"Thousands of airplanes, both heavy bombers and their fighter escorts, flew missions each day, weather permitting. And on each mission they dropped tons of high explosives and incendiary bombs on German factories, military installations, railway systems, and on German cities and towns," Lanier continued. "Bombers like the B-17 Flying Fortress and the B-24 Liberator flew over enemy territory, often at the limits of their endurance. They faced enemy antiaircraft fire, and swarms of enemy fighters."

The flat-screen showed a B-17, its wing afire, as it broke apart and dropped out of the sky.

More footage followed. Of German fighters streaking out of the blue and hammering American aircraft. Of exploding American bombers. Of crippled planes flaming out, most without parachutes blooming forth from their shattered innards.

Another shot of a B-24 spinning out of control, its cockpit burning, graphically illustrated the dangers to the men who had served in the Army Air Corps—as it was called back before the permanent establishment of a separate branch of the service called the United States Air Force.

"Losses among the bomber crews were astronomical," Dr. Lanier said grimly. "For each bomber that went down over enemy territory, ten men were lost or captured."

The image shifted to scenes of Allied prisoners of war behind barbed-wire fences, and a tragic shot of a bomber crewman lying on the ground near the shattered remains of his B-17 bomber.

"Large raids against specific targets—called 'Big Weeks' by the Allied military command—could result in the loss of over a hundred planes in a single five-to-seven-day period." Dr. Lanier paused. "That's over a thousand men dead or captured," he said quietly.

Megan shifted uncomfortably in her seat as she watched the footage and listened to the lecture. While she often dreamed of planning large-scale operations such as this, Megan had seldom computed the human cost of such grandiose missions. But now she was harshly reminded that it was real men and women—not numbers on a mission planning statement—who actually carried out such plans. If she ever achieved her dreams, many of the people she sent into harm's way would return injured, and some wouldn't come back at all.

"Over half a million U.S. aviators served in England during the Second World War," Lanier informed them. "Many of those men never came home."

Matt, Mark, Megan, David, and even Andy Moore were stunned into silence by an image of seemingly endless rows of white crosses—American graves in a French field. More dramatic footage continued to unfold on the flat-screen.

As he watched, Matt thought about his mother, who had spent much of his childhood away from the family, flying fighter planes off aircraft carrier decks. Matt and his father had both missed her terribly. Yet Marissa Hunter's was but a small sacrifice compared to the men who had given their all in the middle of the last century to fight tyranny in one of the longest and most costly wars in human history.

Matt also realized that, like the pilots of the Second World War, his mother lived every day in the certain knowledge that she too could be called to serve—and might not return. That was a scary thought, and Matt immediately turned to face his friend and fellow Net Force Explorer Andy Moore.

Andy Moore lives with that loss every day, Matt realized, trying to read his friend's expression as he listened to the lecture.

In truth, Andy Moore was deeply affected by the dramatic footage, but he made sure it didn't show on his face. Andy didn't want the others to think he was weak.

Up until that moment, the Century of Military Aviation seminar had been a game to him. Andy enjoyed the competition, but the educational aspect of the seminar was of much less interest to him.

But seeing the harrowing films of aircraft plunging out of the sky, knowing that the men inside them were facing certain death—or what was sometimes worse, life as a prisoner of war—reminded Andy that *real* men had given up their lives fighting Nazis over eighty years ago.

And the films also reminded Andy about the very real sacrifice his own father had made for his country. It was something Andy Moore tried not to think about. There wasn't much to be gained, after all, from wondering about what *could* have been.

But sometimes, when he saw Mark with his father, Jay Gridley, or when he watched Matt Hunter interact with his dad, Andy was filled with a terrible sense of loss for the father he'd barely known.

A father who had given his life for his country.

It happened during the uneasy cease-fire after the South African War of 2010–2014. A group of U.S. peacekeepers were attacked and cut off by rebels outside Mandelatown. Rescue choppers were sent in, and a young colonel named Robert Moore supervised the evacuation under merciless enemy fire. Colonel Moore then learned that a platoon of U.S. Rangers had been cut off and surrounded, so he led a group of soldiers into the area to get them out.

In the savage fighting, the platoon was rescued, but resistance was so fierce that someone had to stay behind and cover the platoon's retreat.

That someone was Colonel Robert Moore, Andy's father. He died that day, on that bloody battlefield in Africa.

The loss of his father had left a void in Andy's life that nothing could ever fill. *Everybody says that my dad cared so much for the lives of others, that he gave up his life to save them,* Andy thought sadly. *But Dad probably didn't care about Mom and me. Why else would he die saving a bunch of people he didn't even know?*

How can a father care more about strangers than he does about his own family? he wondered.

Suddenly, Andy Moore noticed Matt Hunter studying him. He quickly pushed his thought aside, before the pain and loss could show on his face.

With an act of will, Andy turned his attention back to Dr. Lanier's lecture.

"By 1943, the tide of the war in Europe had shifted, and the Allied bombers no longer flew alone against the enemy fighters," Dr. Lanier said. "They had their 'Little Friends' to help them."

On the flat-screen, a single-engine fighter streaked past, guns blazing. The images shifted more rapidly now. Shots of wing-camera footage of German planes being knocked out of the sky, the pilot sometimes spinning away from the cockpit at the last possible second, flashed across the gigantic monitor in dramatic silence.

"The first fighter aircraft to arrive at the European theater was the P-47 Thunderbolt," Lanier said as the monitor revealed a stubby, fat-nosed fighter with a four-bladed propeller. "While the Thunderbolt was rugged and effective, its range was limited due to its fuel consumption, and the fighters could not protect the bombers all the way in to the target. Remember," Dr. Lanier reminded them all, "this was before the days of in-flight refueling."

The image shifted again, and Matt, David, and Andy instantly recognized the sleek, trim silver fighter on the screen.

"The P-51 Mustang changed the course of the war," Lanier said. "With large wing tanks for fuel, and drop tanks on its belly, the P-51 could fly from Britain to Poland, a range nearly equaling that of the bombers it protected.''

Again the image shifted, as a variety of aircraft appeared on screen. All of them bore black crosses on their wings and swastikas on their tails.

''Germany did what they could, against insurmountable odds, to counter the threat of the Allies' around-the-clock bombing campaign. The British bombed Germany at night; the Americans bombed Germany in the daylight.''

The image on the screen changed to reveal a sleek German fighter.

''The coming of the Focke-Wulf FW 190 Wurger in 1941 almost changed the course of the war. This plane was as fast and maneuverable as the Mustang, though it was more lightly armed.

''When the Focke-Wulf failed to stem the tide of American and British bombers, more radical designs were tried. Most unsuccessfully.''

A stubby rocket plane appeared on the screen. Its tiny cockpit held a single German pilot, who waved uncomfortably for the cameraman. It was hard to believe that the footage had been taken almost a century before. The pilot had the same nervous expression Matt had seen on his fellow Net Force Explorers before they entered the simulators.

War has a human face, Matt mused. *And it's the same whether it belongs to your friend or your enemy.*

''The Messerschmitt-163 Komet was the most radical of those designs,'' Lanier said. ''A rocket plane with limited range and flight time, over seven hundred Komets were built despite the fact that the fuel they carried was so dangerous and corrosive that many of the airplanes exploded on landing, their pilots' bodies burned away in the massive blast caused by the fuel mixture. Few pilots survived to tell of their experiences aboard a Komet.''

Then the scene shifted again. When a new aircraft appeared on the monitor, Matt recognized it as one of the most important innovations to come out of the Second World War, an invention that would change the face of war in the air forever.

''Near the end of the conflict in Europe, the Mustangs had to deal with their most dangerous threat,'' Lanier continued.

"The Messerschmitt Me-262 was a radical innovation. It was the first jet fighter to fly in combat."

The image shifted again, to a scene of a 262 streaking past a formation of B-24's. One of the bombers exploded, its wing folding under the hammering of the German fighter's six nose guns.

"Wow," David Gray said. "What chance did piston-engine propeller planes have against jets?"

"The Mustang could hold its own," Dr. Lanier said. "Just barely. But fortunately, by that point in the war the Germans could only manufacture a few jets, which were difficult and time-consuming for ground crews to maintain, and even harder to fly."

The image on the screen vanished, and the room lights came back on.

"And fortunately for you, you'll only be dealing with Focke-Wulfs today," Lanier said. "After all, unlike real war, *we* have to be fair."

There were audible sighs of relief all around.

"But there *will* be a few surprises, I assure you," he added ominously.

"I want to say right now that this is one of the most grueling and difficult simulations at the Institute," he said. "The mission takes place in real time—there's no compression in this simulation."

Megan gasped. David Gray rolled his eyes. And Matt recalled Julio's description of the ordeal. He'd conveniently forgotten about this aspect of the simulation.

"This simulation can last up to three hours," Lanier said. "So I suggest you visit the rest rooms before you take off."

Everyone chuckled.

"You have your panic buttons if things get too intense for you," Lanier reminded them. "There is no shame if you use them."

The Net Force Explorers exchanged meaningful glances. They knew that the panic button was not an option for them this mission. Not if they wanted to find Julio.

"Now," the professor concluded. "Off to the simulators, and good luck to you all."

• • •

On the way to the veeyar chamber, Andy Moore stopped to read the roster. He paled and turned to his Net Force Explorers.

"Guess what," he said.

"Don't tell me," David Gray said. "We're going up against Dieter Rosengarten and the Berliners again."

Andy nodded.

"Well," Megan said, "what did you expect? They're pretty well tied to us throughout this first round, either on our side or against us."

"I know what I expect," Andy Moore said. "I expect to kill Dieter. I'm good enough, I'm strong enough. Dieter is meat. *Dead* meat."

Matt turned to Mark, who'd be his wingman for this flight. "Stay close," he said.

Then Matt turned to Andy. "Just don't forget why we're going in there."

Nearly an hour and a half into the veeyar simulation, the Net Force Explorers were suffering from a severe case of boredom. It was an overcast day, though they were flying in the sun above the low-lying clouds. The intermittent cloud cover frequently blocked their view of the landscape below them, so they couldn't spend their time checking for signs of enemy presence or movement on the Continent. One or two of the Net Force Explorers might have drifted off to sleep, if it hadn't been for another factor.

They were also uncomfortable. *Very* uncomfortable. The cockpits of the P-51 Mustangs were cold, despite the pilots' A-1 leather flight jackets, and they were sitting on their parachutes, which was awkward and made for circulation difficulties if they weren't careful. None of them could sleep, even if they wanted to.

Even worse, they'd been ordered to limit their radio contact with each other. Too much chatter could alert the "enemy" to their presence and bring about an early attack.

So there was nothing for the Net Force Explorers to do but fly their planes, keep an eye on their fuel gauges, and search the sky for the enemy. And for Julio.

Matt Hunter checked his wing. Mark Gridley still hung

there, close and tight in the flight pattern, with David Gray and Megan O'Malley high and behind them.

Andy Moore flew well ahead of the rest. He had the lonely job of flying "point" on this mission.

Matt looked over his shoulder and spotted David Gray's distinctive Mustang. David had chosen a Mustang with its tail section painted bright red from the available choices in this simulation. It was the mark of the Tuskeegee Airmen, a group of African-American pilots who flew against the Germans in an all-black squadron.

Megan flew on his wing. Her tail was also painted red, and she had selected a colorful design for the nose of her fighter too. A grinning, evil-looking clown clutching a machine gun.

Matt could see the belly drop tanks strapped to the Mustangs. These tanks carried fuel that extended the Mustang's range. The gas in these tanks was used up first, and the hollow metal cylinders were dropped when empty—or if the planes got into a fight. The exterior fuel tanks were a drag on the airplanes, and dangerously flammable if struck by enemy shells.

Matt's and Mark's Mustangs were less impressive-looking. They'd chosen standard models, with no cosmetic paint. They were here to work, not play. It was their job to survive the sim long enough to find Julio Cortez and talk to him at length, if they could. In the light of their goal, they'd put their energy into practicing, not into modifying their aircrafts' appearance.

Below them in the veeyar, a formation of brown B-17 Flying Fortress bombers approached their target, a German factory complex used for building fighter aircraft. The Net Force Explorers' job was to protect those bombers from Dieter's fighters. But so far, things had been quiet.

That changed suddenly.

Puffs of smoke began exploding all around them, and around the bombers. The tiny explosions, which looked like cotton balls, were the signs of antiaircraft fire from the ground.

Once the barrage started, it would probably continue all the way to the target and back again. It was dangerous and random. An antiaircraft shell could strike their planes at any time, bringing them down. In 1944, Matt knew, flak brought down

3,501 American planes—almost six hundred more planes than German fighters had destroyed.

And they couldn't fight back.

It could be worse, however, as Dr. Lanier had warned them. If the antiaircraft shells suddenly stopped, that meant that the German fighters were on their way.

It was a "lose-lose situation" as far as Matt Hunter could tell.

Matt checked his fuel gauge again. These missions pushed the Mustangs to the limits of their range, even if things went well. If they got into a full-scale scrap now, none of them would have enough fuel to escort the bombers all the way to their targets and then return with them to their base—which was okay in the simulators, but not so great during a real war.

When he noticed his drop tank was empty, Matt reached down and pulled the lever that released it. On his wing, Mark Gridley followed suit.

With their tanks gone, their Mustangs handled a little bit better. Far ahead of them, Matt noticed that Andy Moore had dropped his spare fuel tank as well.

Good, Matt thought with relief. *It looks like Andy is on top of things.*

"Bandits at three o'clock!" David Gray said, startling Matt. But before Matt could even turn his head to the right to scan for the Germans, Megan O'Malley's voice burst through his headphones.

"Bandits at nine o'clock!" she said.

Below them, the formation of bombers was taking hits, too. German Focke-Wulf fighters hiding in the low cloud cover had suddenly erupted from the clouds and were shooting from beneath them, the direction that planes least expected an attack from, using pairs of top-mounted 20-millimeter cannon to fire at them from below. The devastating technique, mostly used for night fighting, was called *Schräge Musik,* "slanting music," the German term at the time for jazz.

"We've got bandits at twelve o'clock," Andy Moore said frantically from ahead of the formation, as German fighters closed in on them.

Trapped! Matt thought. *What do we do now?*

"Going in to engage the enemy," Andy said, showing him

he way. Matt could see his Mustang dive right down onto the ail of an attacking German fighter.

"David, Megan," Matt said. "Take the nine! Mark and I will deal with the others."

Even as he spoke, Matt dipped his wing and banked to the ight to counter the oncoming threat at his three o'clock.

"Heeeere we goooooo!" Mark yelled as he pointed his P-51 at the enemy fighters, who'd broken through the cloud cover and were coming right at them and the bombers they were supposed to defend.

Colonel Stegar stood on top of a low hill, close to the men he was observing, but far enough away to get the "big picture." Partially concealed among some low-hanging branches, the Marine Corps colonel used the digitally enhanced magnification mode of his all-purpose battle visor to observe the team of Navy SEALs he would soon lead into combat.

So far, he liked what he saw.

The seven Navy SEALs were still as fresh as they were when he had parted company with them eight hours ago, despite their two-hour flight on a military transport spaceplane from Washington's Dulles Airport to a small military airfield on the Pacific Coast, and a long ten-"klick" trek through an "environmentally protected" area of undeveloped shoreline in Washington State.

Though the men all knew they were on a "walk in the park," Stegar had made sure that they were outfitted for the trek with full armor, extra ammunition, and all the rations they would need for a two-week mission.

Colonel Stegar wanted the men to get some exercise, and this was their last chance to be physically active for a few days. The next time these "squids" made landfall it would be in enemy territory.

Increasing the magnification on his multi-purpose visor, Stegar noted that the SEALs treated the march quite seriously, despite its routine nature. They traveled with loaded weapons at the ready, as per Stegar's orders, and the colonel saw that they wore also zipknives in their boot sheaths and had an assortment of grenades rigged to their body armor.

One of the seven even carried a Hawkeye antiaircraft missile launcher on his broad back. A nice touch, obviously instigated by Lieutenant Sam Knappert, Stegar's second in command on this mission to Corteguay. Knappert took the job seriously, and communicated that seriousness to the men.

Colonel Stegar had insisted that the SEALs wear full body armor and smartsuits on the march, though he was certain that the SEALs would prefer to save that for the mission. But he wanted them to know he was serious, a heartless Marine Corps command officer, before they set foot in enemy territory.

Well, the colonel reasoned, *they don't have to like me, they just have to obey me.*

Wearing the hot, uncomfortable body armor, smart weapons, and fully computerized and networked helmet with head-up display on what amounted to nothing more than a long endurance march was not really necessary, but Stegar felt it was important anyway. Stegar knew they were used to wearing the irritating head-to-toe clothing and equipment for long hours at a stretch. Now he wanted them used to wearing it at his command.

The colonel also knew that the high-tech DuPont/Rockwell D-1B Battlesuits would be vital to the success of Raptor, which was why he made them wear the suits today, and why he wore one himself.

The suits, usually referred to as smartsuits, were made of a jointed flexible shell of bullet-proof plastic, and could withstand virtually anything but a direct hit from heavy artillery and remain intact, protecting the occupants from most common battle injuries. Smartsuits were the best body armor available, though Colonel Stegar didn't want to test the suits' effectiveness if he could help it. The suits also incorporated superb barriers against chemical and biological weapons.

Available in multiple patterns camouflaged to suit the environment the soldiers expected to encounter, the armor was hard to see with the naked eye. If a soldier was standing still, he looked like a shadow in the brightest daylight, and at night . . .

well, at night the smartsuit and the man wearing it looked like nothing at all.

But the best part of the suit wasn't the protection or camouflage it gave the wearer. The greatest strength of the suit was the advantage it gave the soldiers on the battlefield. A wireless CPU and multiple digital communication devices were embedded in the suit, along with a GPS locator, heat and motion sensors, carriers for multiple weapons, and tiny cameras of various sorts facing in every direction for night, infrared, and ultraviolet vision. The suit's helmet could play views from any of those lenses in a heads-up display on the visor, or overlay those images on computer-generated or real-time satellite-image maps of the battlefield in any scale, complete with notations for the positions of the others in the group, as well as the locations of any known enemy personnel and activity.

The weapons that were a part of the suit could be manually sighted, or could be targeted by using remote feed from the soldier's equipment, satellite links, or commands from a networked HQ. The soldiers had a broad choice of weapons—everything from particle-beam weapons to more primitive projectile rifles right down to a basic field knife, familiar to soldiers for centuries.

Some things just couldn't be improved upon.

While wearing the suit, a soldier could see for great distances in all directions under any conditions—in the dark, in pea-soup fog, or in the pouring rain. He knew exactly where the other members of his team were at all times, and could communicate verbally both with those in the field and with the people back at HQ. He could fire his weapons accurately to demolish the enemy without ever having to physically see his target, and without having to worry about the risks of friendly fire.

Despite the discomfort of being wrapped from head to foot in its shell, American soldiers considered the smartsuit to be one of the greatest inventions of the human race since the wheel.

As the SEALs neared a natural depression in the forest, probably a dried-up streambed, the man on point halted them with a hand signal. This gully would be a perfect place to set up an ambush, and Colonel Stegar was relieved to see that the team was using their training to sniff out danger.

While the colonel watched, the point man and another SEAL silently moved to either side of the trench, slipping through the forest, ready to ambush any waiting ambusher.

Stegar set the visor back to normal vision, and confirmed that his SEALs were nearly invisible in the dappled forest, despite the fact that he knew what to look for and where to look. Any average person without special equipment would have a snowball's chance in the Gobi Desert of seeing his men.

But no matter how well trained and prepared the SEALs were, Colonel Stegar still wondered if they were up to the mission ahead of them. He was torn by doubts at this stage of every special operation he'd ever led, and this one was no different.

Did the service teach them everything they needed to know? Stegar wondered. *Are they good enough to accomplish the mission?*

And are they ready?

Suddenly, Colonel Stegar felt the none-too-gentle pressure of the barrel of a gun on the back of his thick neck.

A soft voice whispered from behind him.

"Password, sir?" it said. The request was punctuated by a little more pressure applied to the muzzle of the gun. The colonel smiled, realizing that he'd been taken totally by surprise.

"Green Tambourine," he whispered.

The gun barrel disappeared. Colonel Stegar turned and faced Lieutenant Samantha "Sam" Knappert, who lowered her weapon and stood at ease. Her blue eyes were shining beneath her visor, but she never even cracked a smile of triumph.

"Good to see you again, Colonel," she said, as if they'd just run into each other at the local mall.

Yes, Stegar thought with a rush of satisfaction. *They're ready . . . .*

Matt Hunter snapped his P-51 into a steep barrel roll, diving among the German fighters while his plane twisted through the air like a corkscrew. Mark Gridley was on his wing, and he turned with Matt, move for move. At the end of the barrel roll, Mark banked his fighter to the right even as Matt, his wingman, broke left.

In the chaos of battle, and the tangle of fighters and bombers, Mark and Matt quickly lost sight of one another—a huge mistake because a two-plane team was vastly more effective in air combat than a single plane. But, Matt knew, there was very little he could do about it at this moment.

Matt leveled off again. Almost immediately, he spotted a Focke-Wulf hammering away at a B-17. Matt pushed the throttle forward, after quickly checking his six to make sure no one got behind him.

Matt reached the Focke-Wulf even as the German killed his target. With a fiery, roiling cloud of burning fuel, the B-17's wing exploded and collapsed. The bomber tilted and literally fell out of the sky in an almost straight line to the virtual landscape below.

As the German banked away from its kill, it unknowingly flew directly into Matt's path. At the last second, the German pilot spotted Matt's Mustang coming at him. He pulled up, exposing the Focke-Wulf's soft underbelly to Matt's guns.

Without hesitation, Matt depressed the trigger. The German plane detonated with the first burst. A chunk of wing broke free, followed by a landing wheel and strut. Matt jinked his plane, narrowly avoiding flying into the German's debris.

One less, Matt thought grimly. *The more Germans we kill, the sooner we can talk to Julio.*

Mark Gridley, meanwhile, was on the tail of another German. He fired a two-second burst, but missed.

Suddenly, tracers tore out of the sky behind him. One shell ripped into his Mustang's wing, and the whole fighter shuddered as a chunk of aluminum broke loose and was swept away in the slipstream. For a second, Mark hesitated. He pulled back on the stick, stunned by the suddenness of the attack.

It was that one-second hesitation that saved Mark. As his Mustang slowed, the German in front of him was able to jink away and make his escape. But the Focke-Wulf that was on his tail flashed right past him because the pilot assumed Mark was dead in the air. Now the tables were turned. The hunter became the hunted.

Heedless of the damage to his aircraft, Mark Gridley pushed his throttle forward and chased the German in front of him. When the fighter dipped into his sights, Mark fired.

His bullets danced up the German's tail, along his fuselage, and next to the gas tank. The Focke-Wulf seemed to melt into a rolling cloud of smoke and fire. Mark flew right through the debris and burst out on the other side.

The sky was clear ahead of him. Mark turned, and saw that he was flying away from the formation. He looped around and headed back to rejoin the battle. But as he did, he saw a flash of sunlight reflected off cockpit glass out of the corner of his eye.

Mark squinted into the sun. What he saw diving at him made Mark Gridley's blood run cold.

It can't be! Mark's mind screamed.

Then they were on him. . . .

Megan was having one of her best days in the veeyar simulators ever.

Though she quickly lost sight of David, her wingman, she went up against the Germans boldly and alone. When she saw two Focke-Wulfs strafing a bomber, she turned right into their path. Megan knew that there was nothing she could do to help the bomber, which was already streaming smoke from a dozen hits. But Megan was heartened to see that the Germans hadn't been able to inflict enough damage to down the B-17. With one engine burning, the bomber dipped out of the formation and turned back to base.

That meant that the bomber was coming toward Megan. She smiled with predatory glee. *If these Germans are kill-happy, then they'll follow this cripple to try and finish her off. Boy, will they be surprised to find me waiting for them. . . .*

Unfortunately, one of the German fighters broke away from the stricken bomber, but the other continued after the wounded airplane. Megan ducked under the belly of the American bomber—hoping that the virtual gunners in the B-17 would recognize her Mustang as a friend and not a foe.

Luckily, that was just what happened.

As the German swooped in for the kill, the "sitting duck" produced a baby hawk from under its wing. Megan opened up with the Mustang's nose cannon.

Less than three seconds later the German plane was spinning toward the earth. Megan watched as the pilot of the stricken Focke-Wulf opened his cockpit and leaped clear, spinning wildly until the parachute blossomed above him.

What a nut! Megan said to herself, admiring the German student's guts. *I would have just hit the panic button.* Megan circled the area, watching her kill.

Though a fighter falling out of the sky is a graceful and awesome sight, it is not wise to linger on the vision for long, as Megan soon discovered. She didn't even see the fighter that killed her.

One minute, Megan O'Malley was sitting in the cockpit over Europe. The next, she was disoriented and blinking in the veeyar chamber.

"The German student you took out wanted me to pass on a comment—he was impressed by your shooting," Professor Lanier said.

But for Megan, who'd failed in her ultimate mission, that wasn't enough to ease the sting of not surviving until the end of the simulation.

David Gray saw Megan's plane explode as he was trying to catch up with her. He didn't see the fighter that killed her either . . . not at first. But then, as the debris of her P-51 fell from the sky in a burning fireball, a Focke-Wulf shot past the wreckage, toward a bomber below.

David had no time for regrets. He had tried and failed to save Megan—it was as simple as that. As far as David Gray knew, he was the only Net Force Explorer left in the veeyar. He wanted to live as long as possible, to give Julio Cortez the chance to make an appearance.

So far, so good, he thought. But as he banked his wing and flipped over into a steep dive to catch the German, David remembered to check his six.

He was glad he did, because a sky-blue Focke-Wulf with a ferocious tiger face painted on its nose was coming right at his bright red tail. He recognized the paint scheme on the

German fighter instantly. It was a variation of the design the same pilot had on his Fokker triplane.

Dieter Rosengarten is on my tail, David realized.

Wildly, he searched for something to do to shake this demon of veeyar off his butt. In near panic, he moved directly toward the formation of bombers, hoping to jink among the larger planes and lose the German on his tail.

But as David came around one B-17, another, wounded by a German fighter, dropped right into his path. David pulled back on the throttle and just missed hitting the bomber, which continued to drop out of the sky as chunks of its burning engines fell away behind it.

Miraculously, the Focke-Wulf that got Megan was still in front of him. No doubt the German had been the one to kill the Flying Fortress that David had almost rammed a moment ago.

David forgot about Dieter Rosengarten. He pressed the trigger, and his Mustang shuddered as hundreds of rounds of ammunition poured out of his wings. The German fighter in front of him spun away, its wing in tatters.

Then David's Mustang shook as shells from Dieter Rosengarten's Focke-Wulf struck it. Bullets pounded his tail fin and danced along his fuselage as David fought for control of his dying airplane. . . .

When Matt downed his second German, he climbed above the bombers and searched the sky for his wingman.

What he saw shocked and frightened him.

In the distance, Mark Gridley's Mustang was being attacked by two German fighters—Messerschmitt Me-262 *jet* fighters.

This isn't supposed to happen! Matt thought. *Somebody's cheating!* But then Matt realized that the German students probably had nothing to do with the jet fighters being here.

These mysterious bandits might just come from the same place as Julio, he thought with mounting panic. *Virtual guard dogs who hacked into the system to drag their prisoner back.*

Matt pushed the throttle forward, glancing at his fuel gauge for the first time in many minutes.

Not enough, he thought grimly. *I guess I'll never make it back to base. But maybe I can save Mark!*

• • •

Mark Gridley still couldn't believe his eyes. Not until the nose cannons on one of the 262's spat lead at him did he react. Then his first action was to curse his mistake.

Mark jinked, twisting his Mustang in the sky to avoid the German jets. The first one flashed right by him, and Mark could see the strange and unconventional markings on it. Instead of German crosses or swastikas, the overall color scheme on the Me-262 was black. But on its tail fin Mark recognized the symbol for the terrorist group Cuba Libre.

He knew then that something was very, very wrong. Mark got on the horn instantly, breaking their radio silence.

"Mayday! Mayday!" he said. "To all the Net Force Explorers. We have bandits in the simulator. *Real* bandits!"

At that moment, the second Messerschmitt Me-262 roared toward him, and this pilot's aim was much better. Mark felt his Mustang shudder; then the propeller shattered.

Just then, Mark heard Matt reply to his frantic warning and distress call. "On my way," Matt said.

Mark touched his radio. "Too late—" Then he was gone.

Like Megan, Mark found himself abruptly back in the real world. In veeyar, his airplane broke apart while Matt watched helplessly.

Andy Moore saw David's plane explode, and he saw the culprit responsible for downing his friend a split second later.

Dieter Rosengarten!

This was it for Dieter, Andy decided. He twisted and banked his airplane and flew right toward the sky-blue Focke-Wulf. Since he was already above and behind Rosengarten's fighter, Andy managed to get on the German's tail without too much trouble.

At that moment, Andy Moore heard Mark's enigmatic radio call. But he didn't have time to think about it now. Andy was almost in the kill position.

Andy Moore squinted through his gun sight. Then, with calm deliberation, he depressed the trigger. Tracers streaked through the sky, striking Dieter's wing.

Andy was peeved that he didn't down the German then and there. But he was rewarded when he saw the German's obvious panic. Rosengarten jinked his airplane, not knowing precisely where the attack was coming from, and Andy was able to easily match the German's every twist and turn.

But when Dieter Rosengarten leveled off for a second, Andy Moore saw past the German's Focke-Wulf, and spotted another, more serious dogfight in progress.

Matt Hunter watched helplessly as Mark Gridley's aircraft was blown out of the sky. Almost immediately, the two Me-262's formed up and he got a good look at the strange aircraft.

They were 262's, all right. The planes had the traditional swept-back wings of early jet fighters, and two large, cylindrical engines hanging under each wing, the jet engines.

One of the 262's was all black. The other was white with red stripes running along the fuselage and wings. Matt was startled to discover that the paint scheme was the traditional "Rising Sun," the symbol of Imperial Japan during the Second World War. Matt barely absorbed those details when both fighters banked and came right at him?

Oh, no, he thought. *What do I do now?*

Andy Moore had less than a second to make a decision. Should he take down Dieter Rosengarten, or should he rescue Matt from the two jet fighters that were coming right at him?

To his own surprise, Andy Moore didn't even hesitate. He broke away from Dieter's Focke-Wulf and turned into the path of the two Messerschmitts. His angle of attack was poor, Andy realized, and the jets were coming much too fast for him to swing his nose around and train his guns on them.

Andy Moore gritted his teeth, and twisted the joystick.

As the black jet fighter loomed in his cockpit windshield, Andy Moore had time to scream a shout of rage and frustration.

Matt couldn't believe his good fortune. One minute, he was dead meat, with two jet fighters coming at him in formation.

The next second a Mustang appeared out of nowhere and slammed into the black fighter. The explosion was very powerful—it rocked Matt's Mustang so much he had to fight for control.

The blast was also powerful enough to engulf the second jet fighter. That plane too exploded, lending its fuel to the spreading fire in the sky.

Matt knew that he owed that Net Force Explorer his thanks.

Cautiously, Matt leveled off, then checked his fuel gauge. He would have to punch out soon enough. The Mustang was running on less than half a tank. Carefully, Matt scanned the sky, searching for Julio—hoping that his friend would appear.

Suddenly, the familiar voice crackled in his headphones.

"Matt, *mi amigo*," Julio Cortez said. "I am here again."

Matt Hunter dipped his wing, and then he saw Julio. His friend was flying an orange, tiger-stripped, twin-engine P-38 Lightning.

"*Jefe!*" Matt said. "We have to talk!"

"Time is running out, my friend," Julio Cortez said to Matt, his voice weak and labored.

They flew their veeyar aircraft side by side in the simulator. Off to the left and high above them, the B-17 bombers began to drop their payload of bombs on a rail yard far below. Explosions sprouted on the ground like mushrooms.

Matt knew he shouldn't relax his guard—after his experience with the two jets, he knew that anybody and anything could still be in the sim and gunning for him. Nonetheless, Matt turned toward his friend. He could see Julio through the cockpit of his P-38. He looked haggard and tired, as if great effort were required just to manifest himself.

This is no Rift, Matt knew. Julio was real, and Matt was determined to do what he could to help Julio and his family.

"How did you come here, *Jefe*?" he asked. "How is such a thing possible?"

Julio shook his head. "I don't know, Matt," he said. "The place they put us in, it is a virtual prison. Our minds as well as our bodies are trapped. Do you remember reading in school about the Russian sleep programs used to brainwash political prisoners at the end of the last century? I think my captors decided to see if they worked. To pull off the scam they are planning on election day, they need my family to cooperate with them, so they're trying to shape us to their will."

"Then how did you manage to escape?" Matt asked.

"It was very hard at first," Julio said. "When we were hooked up to the computer, my mind was in chaos. The computer links our captors forced upon us tried to overwhelm my consciousness. I couldn't form a coherent thought; simple mental tasks were impossible. But then . . ."

"What, Julio?" Matt said. "Tell me!"

"I . . . I thought about flying, Matt," Julio said. "It was the thing I loved best in the world. Gradually I came back to myself. And when I did, I remembered these simulators, and it occurred to me that I knew where you would be, and what you would be doing. The government was sending hourly updates to the U.N. with reports on the election. If I could just get access to those signals, I could piggyback and use them to break into the IEI. I knew their systems and simulators, and was sure that if I could just break into a sim, we could talk.

"You were the only person I could think of who'd listen to me, who would believe without questioning in such a wild story. My jailers had plugged me into a neural net for dreadful reasons of their own. All I had to do then was turn their weapon into mine. The worst problem I faced was that the computers that they hooked us up to in order to brainwash us were dedicated systems, not connected to the Net. Then I realized something. The prison had no phones lines of any sort running into it, and Corteguay's mountains made direct radio transmission to the capital city impossible. I knew that these men must have a way to speak with their masters in Adello. Finally I found a way to piggyback onto the communications signal that they beam up and bounce off a satellite.

"Somehow, that discovery seemed to break the spell their brainwashing attempts had held over me. I began to think more clearly. Finally, I got myself into here, with you and the other Net Force Explorers."

"And then you came back," Matt whispered.

"Each time I did it became easier," Julio continued. "I had trouble entering certain systems, the ones that I'd never experienced before, but almost always, when I was in a system I knew well, I found you."

"Can you help me drag in somebody in the government here to help you?" Matt asked. "We need real proof of what is going on with you—we've tried to talk to officials about this already, and failed to get anywhere. They won't believe us until they have undeniable evidence, and they get to decide what constitutes undeniable."

"I don't know if I can give that kind of proof to you." Julio paused. "I can tell you more about where my family and I are being held. Will that help you?"

Julio described the installation, its functions, and its location in detail. Matt strived to memorize it all.

"Are you certain?" Matt asked as Julio finished.

"As certain as I *can* be, Matt," his friend said. "I took a virtual tour of the prison. I saw the outside of it through the surveillance system, and I explored the virtual bars of my prison as well. I have seen the guards. And once I saw my uncle, Mateo, drive through the prison gates, though I never saw the warden who runs the prison."

"Then I can tell Net Force. The State Department," Matt said. "The military can mount a rescue!"

"NO!" Julio said.

"But why not?" Matt asked, confused.

Julio paused. "It would mean certain death for me and my family," he said. "The hookup that keeps us prisoner has a fail-safe system. The jailers can run thousands of volts of electricity through our bodies with the touch of a button at any time, or automatically if the prison's security is breached. No rescuers could ever hope to reach us in time."

"Then what can we . . . what can *I* do, *Jefe*?" Matt asked.

"I think I can turn off the computer program that imprisons us, Matt," Julio said. "I think I can neutralize the surveillance system and the computer locks too."

"That's great!" Matt said. "I'll tell your rescuers everything you tell me. We're gonna get you out of there. Look, Dr. Lanier is probably going to pull the plug on this simulator pretty soon. So we don't have much time, Julio," Matt said. "And I have a question—who are those guys in the jet fighters?"

"Prison guards," Julio said. "They're trying to trace me every time I go on line. The last time a security program increased the brainwashing feed and brought me back to the prison. But the jailers never found out how I escaped, so they couldn't stop me this time either—or, hopefully, the next.''

"But that was no surveillance program that came after you today!" Matt said. "Those jets had human guidance."

"You are correct, my friend," Julio said. "My jailer has found another way to torment me. Somehow, maybe through Uncle Mateo, he has discovered where I go, and sends these men to overpower us before we can talk."

"What can I do, Julio?" Matt asked again. "Tell me."

"You have to find out if your people, your military, are coming to rescue us, Matt," Julio said. "If I know when they are coming, I can return to the prison and deactivate the programs, free my family, and let the rescuers into the prison by shutting down the surveillance system. Then all they will have to deal with is the human guards."

"But—"

"There is no other way!" Julio said. "And this must be done soon, Matt. Time is running out."

Matt peered through his cockpit window. His plane had flown on for a long time, but the sim could end at any moment. *We're all running out of time*, Matt thought frantically.

"What's the hurry on your end?" Matt asked.

"My sister," Julio said. "Juanita . . . she is very sick. She has a fever. The care in the prison is not good."

Oh, no. Matt thought about the little girl who used to bedevil her big brother, and Matt too, when he visited.

"You can count on me," Matt promised. "I'll get a rescue team mobilized, and I'll have all the information you could need or want about how and when. But how can I let *you* know what I've discovered?"

Julio smiled for the first time since he appeared in the veeyar.

"I'll find you," he said confidently. "The Bosnia simulation is next, is it not?"

Matt smiled too. "Then we'll meet in the Bosnian scenario, *Jefe*," Matt said. "We'll be there. But try to come sooner."

"I will see you then, my friend," Julio said, his voice fading fast.

Matt Hunter watched as Julio's airplane began to fade too.

"Wait!" he said, reluctant to see his friend go.

But as Matt watched, the black and orange P-38 vanished.

Matt Hunter turned his attention back to his own aircraft. As he peered out of his cockpit window, he realized his concentration on Julio had nearly cost him his virtual life. He was in a dive he couldn't possibly pull out of. The earth rushed up to meet him. Virtual death was staring him in the face, but Matt hardly noticed. His mind was in turmoil.

How can I do what I promised Julio I would do? he wondered. *And what will happen if I fail?*

Just before the P-51 Mustang struck the ground, Matt saw Dieter's wounded plane, flying still but not maneuvering to destroy him—possibly because Matt was doing such a good job of it on his own. Matt hit the panic button, and was gone.

Mateo knew something was wrong as soon as he approached the gate to the installation in his battered Hummer. The Cuban guards were incredibly vigilant this time, and instead of opening the gate to wave him through, the Cuban sergeant in charge of security came out through the narrow door in the fence to check Mateo's vehicle personally.

When Mateo asked what was wrong, the Cuban just shrugged his shoulders and waved him through the gate.

The guards inside the compound all had a harried, hunted look about them, and Mateo upgraded from worry to panic.

When he exited the elevator on the main floor of the underground complex, Mateo felt as if he'd entered a new, ultramodern circle of Dante's Hell. But not even that celebrated Italian poet could have imagined the nightmarish scene that confronted him.

The first sound he heard was a terrible, demented moaning—a continuous sound of mortal agony. Mateo turned and saw the Cuban assassin. He was lying on the floor in stained and ragged clothes. Blood had dried on his scalp from a cruel wound. Mateo saw that the man was clutching something to his chest protectively. Cautiously, he approached the man.

The Cuban was clutching his Drex-Dream reservoir. Or rather, the shattered *remains* of it. Someone had smashed it, and nearly smashed the Cuban's skull as well.

Mateo turned, and almost jumped out of his skin.

He hadn't noticed the Yakuza assassin. But the man was there, in the shadows, sitting in a lotus position. His face was impassive, as always, but there were marks of a beating on his face and neck.

Another moan came from the man on the ground. Mateo did not look. Instead, he crossed the underground chamber to check on the prisoners.

Mateo almost stumbled over another body on the floor. But this one wasn't moving, or making a sound. Mateo checked on the crumpled form at his feet.

It was the slovenly woman who took care of the prisoners' physical needs. This woman was dead.

"We had a small excitement while you were in the capital, my friend," his master said from behind Mateo.

Mateo turned to face the older man. The master was staring at him, but he was not smiling.

"Your nephew attempted to escape again," the master said. "I sent my assassins to bring him back."

The master cast a cold eye on the man moaning on the floor, and the Japanese meditating in the corner.

"They failed," he said. "And so they had to be punished."

Mateo heard the Cuban whimper, and he tried to shut out the sound of pure human agony that burst from the assassin's battered lips.

"At least the Yakuza was contrite," the master continued. "He offered me his little finger by way of apology—it is *giri*—his duty." The master laughed, and the sound chilled Mateo to his very soul.

"I told him to keep his finger," the master continued. "I warned the Japanese that if he failed me again, I would take a more important piece of him . . . perhaps his heart."

The master then cast his eye on the whimpering form of the Cuban. He pointed.

"This pig, however, did not have enough honor to even apologize," the master said, kicking the man on the floor. The Cuban curled up into a ball and continued to moan.

"So I destroyed his little toy."

Mateo, sick and disgusted by the spectacle, turned away from the two assassins.

"Is there any word on a possible raid?" Mateo asked.

The master nodded. "Undoubtedly," he said, "they will come. But according to my intelligence sources, the Norteamericanos still think that your brother and his family are in the concentration camp. They will not come here."

Mateo wanted to point out that, with all the increased activity at this facility, with trucks coming from the capital city of Adello every day, the Americans might well have taken notice of this place. But he said nothing.

Mateo was well conditioned not to question the judgment of the man who owned him.

"The raid will come soon, Mateo," the master said, staring off into space. "And I have laid a trap for them. Corteguay is but a tiny nation. And yet, through my genius, we will humble the Americans, and kill and capture even more of their agents of insurrection and chaos."

"But what about the boy?" Mateo asked. "Did he try to contact his friends in the Net Force Explorers?"

"What could he tell them even if he did?" the master said. "That he is a prisoner? The Norteamericanos know that already, though they have decided, for their own reasons, to go along with our charade. Even if he did contact his friends, who would believe them? What can he tell them? How can Julio know where he is being held?" his master asked. "How can he help himself, or his family?" The master shook his head and smiled. "Do not worry, Mateo," he concluded. "There is no hope for your brother and his family. None."

Suddenly, Mateo heard another sound. The cry of a little child, moaning in pain or discomfort.

He turned and stared in the direction of the prisoners. They were still arranged on their implant tables, still hooked up to the computers that confined them.

Mateo approached the tables.

The American soldiers were still entranced, and were at peace.

These men are lucky that they don't know how they smell, Mateo thought as he covered his mouth with a handkerchief. *Or how their bodies are wasting away from inactivity.*

Mateo checked on his brother and his wife. They too seemed peaceful, though their bodies were filthy and they were showing the first signs of wastage.

Next Mateo checked on his niece and nephew. Julio was locked in some struggle, if his tense facial expression was any indication of what his mind was experiencing. He seemed to be fighting the programming constantly, and the effort made him appear weak and haggard.

Then Mateo saw the little girl. Juanita was her name. The child's body was covered with a thin sheen of perspiration, and her usually pale skin was flushed. Mateo touched her neck. Her skin was burning to the touch, and the vibro-mattress was hot underneath her.

He turned back to his master.

"The little one is sick," he said. The master turned to Mateo, but seemed annoyed at the interruption.

"It is of no consequence," his master said before moving off to another part of the facility, two Cuban guards in tow.

Alone with his brother's family, Mateo was also alone with his conscience.

Funny, he thought as he gazed at the suffering child. *I thought I lost my conscience a long time ago.*

Mateo turned and located the metal pan that the dead woman had used to bathe her charges. He turned to the Japanese assassin.

"You!" Mateo barked. "Get up."

The Japanese man turned his head. Then he slowly rose and approached the prisoners. Mateo thrust the pan into the Yakuza's hand.

"Find me some cool water and a sponge," Mateo said.

When the assassin returned a few minutes later, he handed Mateo Cortez a full pan and a clean sponge. As Mateo began to bathe the feverish little girl, the Japanese returned to his lotus position in the corner of the room and resumed his meditation, heedless of anything, or anyone, around him.

Colonel Stegar, Lieutenant Knappert, and the rest of the SEALs were stowed away below deck. The crew of the "cargo ship" had made them as comfortable as possible, considering the cramped spaces.

The team was aboard what appeared to be an old container ship that routinely plied the South and Central American coastlines and the islands of the Caribbean.

The ship made its regular run with a cargo of cheap consumer goods from America, which were then sold to distrib-tors all over Latin America. Along the way it picked up local trade goods, and it was due quite shortly to pass the island of Corteguay, nestled against the South American Pacific coastline.

The cargo ship, christened *Misty Water,* was a frequent sight on that coast, and the Corteguan Navy—what there was of it—hardly noted its passing. The ship hadn't been hailed by patrol boats sent out by the socialist government in many months.

The captain was sure that the cargo tub had been all but forgotten by the Corteguans because it was such a part of the landscape, moving just off their coast on its regular run.

Little did the Corteguans know that the *Misty Water* was more than a mere cargo carrier. In truth, it was a United States Navy intelligence ship, outfitted with top-of-the-line electronic spy and surveillance equipment, and manned by a highly trained and dedicated crew of professional officers.

Inside its artfully rusted hull, the *Misty Water* also had underwater hatches that were used in covert operations. The ship could lazily pass an enemy coast while invisibly sending out strike teams that could sabotage coastal defense systems—as it had done on its last pass by the Corteguan coast a few weeks before.

The *Misty Water* could also be used to place SEAL teams near their objectives, and drop them off without observers being the wiser, which was its mission this time.

Colonel Stegar and Lieutenant Knappert were under the deck in the space they used as a mission planning area. It had a map station, satellite linkups, and computers, but not much space.

In those cramped and musty quarters, the colonel grilled his SEALs and reviewed their mission with them again and again, until he was satisfied that they knew their job and were ready to do it.

One such briefing had just ended. Colonel Stegar decided that it would be the last. It was time for him to let his men rest.

Colonel Stegar checked the mission clock on his wrist. In less than four hours, they would exit the underwater hatch and, using high-tech underwater gear, swim to the shore of Corteguay under the cover of night.

It would be a dangerous time. The defenses that were sab-
otaged last trip might have been repaired without their knowing it. Or a casual fisherman strolling on the beach might se
them as they emerged from the ocean.

Stegar knew that a thousand things could go wrong.

And that was only the *first* phase of the mission calle
Raptor. . . .

14

The post-veeyar briefing with Dr. Lanier was mercifully short.

As far as any of the Net Force Explorers knew, none of the other participants saw the mysterious jet fighters in the simulation. And, of course, none of the Net Force Explorers mentioned it outside the group. It remained their secret.

As had been the case before, a Rift had formed and crashed the simulator, so that Lanier and his techs were too busy trying to figure out what was wrong with their computer to worry about Matt and his friends.

After the briefing, when the holoform Germans visited the Net Force Explorers in the IEI briefing room, Matt couldn't help but notice that Dieter Rosengarten was looking at him strangely.

Could Dieter have seen something? Matt wondered. *Like oddly painted Messerschmitt Me-262's that weren't supposed to be there—or a mysterious orange airplane?*

And when Matt and Dieter finally met holo-to-face, Dieter was polite, but Matt sensed that a question was hovering in the air between them. A question Matt hoped that the German wouldn't ask.

After the debrief and the reception for the Germans, the Net Force Explorers headed back to IEI Lounge. Matt had called an emergency meeting.

As soon as they arrived at the Lounge, Matt put in a call

to the Director's office. They were informed that Jay Gridley was in a meeting with the Speaker of the House of Representatives, but he would be there shortly.

Matt decided to convene the meeting without the Director.

His first act after the meeting began surprised everyone. Matt turned to Andy Moore and put his hand on the other's shoulder.

"Whatever happens next," Matt said, "we owe it all to you, Andy."

None of the other Net Force Explorers had a clue as to what happened after they were knocked out of the running, so Matt told them about Andy giving up his chance to take down Dieter Rosengarten to come to Matt's aid. He explained how Andy had rammed the mysterious jet planes to bring them down, which took *him* out too.

"If you hadn't done that, I would never have been able to talk to Julio," Matt explained. "You saved the day, Andy."

"Wow," David Gray said, slapping Andy on the back. "I know how much you wanted to shoot down Dieter Rosengarten. You did good, my man!"

"It takes a real man to sacrifice himself for the good of another," Megan O'Malley added.

"I can't believe that you had Baron von Dieter on the run!" Mark Gridley said.

But it was Megan who spoke the words that made Andy feel truly special. After the others had congratulated him, she stepped up to Andy and looked into his eyes.

"Your father would be proud of you," she said simply.

Andy Moore was too surprised to say anything then. He accepted the acclaim and Megan's heartfelt words with awkward humility. He even blushed.

The often abrasive Andy just wasn't used to praise, and he didn't know how to handle it.

A few moments later, Andy was rescued from his uncomfortable position as a hero by the arrival of Director Jay Gridley, with another agent in tow.

"Sorry I'm late," he said, getting down to business at once. "Now tell me, what have you got?"

Matt took a deep breath, then he closed his eyes. *Here goes,* he thought. Then he told them all he had learned. . . .

. . .

Matt Hunter was not happy with the Director's solutions.

Matt had told the head of Net Force, along with the rest of the Net Force Explorers, everything Julio had said in the veeyar simulator. As he related the story, Matt groped to recall every tiny detail. While Matt spoke, Jay Gridley recorded it all.

When Matt was finished, he looked at Jay Gridley expectantly, hoping that the director could suggest a course of action to solve this dilemma.

Unfortunately, Matt had been disappointed.

Instead of offering solutions, the Director insisted that they stay the course at the Institute, and keep to the same strategy as before. The Net Force Explorers were supposed to remain silent about what was happening, and wait for the Director to contact the State Department, the military, or whoever else needed to be informed.

It was a bureaucratic answer, not the answer Matt Hunter wanted to hear.

After admonishing them all to keep what they'd learned a secret, Jay Gridley left the Lounge. Soon after, Matt adjourned the meeting.

As everyone prepared to depart, Mark Gridley approached his friend.

"What are you going to do now?" Mark asked.

Matt sighed. "I'm not sure," he said guardedly.

Matt knew that if he went against Jay Gridley's wishes, then he didn't want the director's own son implicated in any wrongdoing. It was Matt's way of protecting his young friend.

Mark seemed to understand without having it explained to him. He nodded, and spoke.

"I just wanted to say that I will support your decision," Mark said, "as a Net Force Explorer and as your friend, no matter what you decide."

Matt was grateful for the vote of confidence, but he knew he had to take the next step on his own.

"Matt!" his mother said when she returned home. "It's after midnight, what are you doing up so late?"

Matt met his mother's eyes. "I have to talk to you, Mom,"

he said. Marissa Hunter blinked, and Matt could tell that his mother was uncomfortable. Again, he suspected she was hiding something.

"It's about Julio." Matt said, tripping over his words in his haste to get the truth out. "I saw him again. In the veeyar."

Marissa Hunter visibly paled, and Matt's suspicions were all but confirmed.

I have to level with her, Matt decided. *It's the only way. I can't expect the truth from her if I don't admit everything.*

Matt took a deep breath, sat down opposite his mother, and told her the whole story, from the beginning.

When Matt finished, they both sat together in silence.

Matt sensed that he'd somehow put his mother into a compromising position, though he wasn't sure quite how. But he was sure that she could do *something* to save his friend. She worked in the Pentagon, after all.

It was the only hope Matt had to cling to. . . .

He saw his mother hesitate, as though torn between conflicting loyalties, or maybe unable to decide what the proper course of action was. Then, all of a sudden, she relaxed. Whatever was bugging her, she'd finally made up her mind what to do about it.

She reached out and took his hand in hers. "I have something to tell you, Matt," she said.

At that very moment, thousands of miles away, nine people in scuba gear slipped out of the Pacific Ocean and crawled across a darkened beach in Corteguay.

One by one the SEALs emerged from the cool ocean, carrying huge waterproof bundles of weapons and equipment. As Colonel Stegar dragged his own equipment ashore and ducked into a line of trees, he checked his digital wristwatch.

When he saw the dully glowing numbers displayed, he cursed inwardly.

They were already sixteen minutes behind schedule.

The delay had been unavoidable. The SEAL team had had to linger underwater while a heavily armed Corteguan patrol boat motored toward the *Misty Water*. When the colonel saw the captain of the Corteguan vessel hail the cargo ship, he got worried.

With his head just above the surface of the waves, and using the high-tech scuba helmet to amplify the voices of the men on the boats, Stegar heard all that transpired. He watched, wondering if the patrol crew would linger near the beach long enough to end their mission then and there.

Stegar breathed a sigh of relief when he realized that the patrol boat was out tonight in the hope of trading black market goods with the crew of the *Misty Water*. Stegar listened as the crew of the cargo ship haggled in Spanish with the men on the patrol boat. In the end, some goods and some real currency—not electronic transactions—were exchanged.

Then the patrol craft sped off into the night, probably looking for more customers for their black market stash. When they were out of sight, Stegar led his men to shore, as the *Misty Water* idled in the distance.

At this point in the mission, they started stripping off their scuba gear. One of the crewmen off the *Misty Water,* also a SEAL, had come ashore with them. His job was to drag their scuba gear back to the ship with him. If for some reason they needed to do a sea evacuation instead of the planned helicopter pickup, he would bring it back to the beach at their signal. This gave the SEALs a couple of escape options and improved their chances of remaining undetected.

While the men donned their smartsuits and readied their equipment and weapons for the long jungle march, the sailor from the cargo ship packed their scuba gear up in the waterproof bags for the return trip.

"Good luck, Colonel," the sailor whispered when he was finished. "I wish I was going with you."

Stegar shook the man's hand. Then the crewman slipped back into the ocean, dragging the gear behind him. In seconds he vanished beneath the waves, without even a ripple to mark his passing.

The SEAL team was ready to go, so Stegar rose from the sand.

"Let's pull out," he whispered. "Knappert, Connolly. You're on point."

As one, the soldiers moved into position and melted into the dark jungle.

•   •   •

Matt listened as his mother told him about the Raptor file.

The SEAL team is already in Corteguay, Matt thought, and the anxiety he'd felt since he'd seen Julio in the simulator for the first time reached a fever pitch. Then he turned to his mother.

"Is there any way to stop the attack, or delay it a day or so?" he asked. She shook her head.

"Every second those men are in enemy territory they are in danger," she told her son. "They could abort if they had to, but that would be the end of it. The mission goes off now, before the election in Corteguay, or not at all," she concluded.

Then it has to be now, Matt thought.

"Can we talk to them, get a message to them?"

"I don't know. I doubt it. I imagine they're observing radio silence throughout the course of the mission, but I can find out for you if you need to know for sure."

"I think that would be a good idea," Matt said.

He checked the timetable of the attack again. When he was finished calculating everything, including the time differences between Washington and Corteguay, Matt knew that there would be a little time to warn Julio, but not much.

And if he, or someone else, failed to contact Julio in the Bosnian scenario, then the raid on the secret prison would go down without Julio knowing it was coming—which, by Julio's own account, would result in his death, and the death of his entire family.

The responsibility was crushing.

And there wasn't enough time to do this right.

If they had IEI's cooperation, Matt or somebody official could go alone into that simulator and warn Julio without interference from a bunch of people fighting war games.

But if the past week was any example of the speed with which diplomatic negotiations took place, getting that cooperation was an impossible dream.

Net Force, or even Matt and his friends, could crash the simulators. They'd done that before. But they couldn't co-opt them without the full consent of IEI. And Matt, after trying to get the world to listen to him for more than a week, was sure that nobody, not even the whole U.S. government, could get that consent in time.

If they didn't get it, Matt would have to do what he'd done for the last two weeks. Go to class, beat world-class competition, and hope that he'd find Julio. But this time, Julio's life, and the lives of every prisoner in the virtual prison, depended on him.

Without Net Force to work a miracle, it was up to Matt Hunter. Matt, and the other Net Force Explorers.

When we go into that simulator again, it will be real, Matt realized. *As real as any war can be. If we fail, human beings will die.*

His mother came up behind him and put her hand on his shoulder.

"I never thought you'd be in this position," she said. "I've worked my whole life to try to make sure you'd never be embroiled in a shooting war. Even though I know you'll be safe in that simulator, Julio is in terrible trouble. I hate that."

"I know," Matt said.

"I've watched you this last week. Your friend was in danger, and you did everything you could to save him. Even when I thought you were wrong about what was going on, I could see how dedicated you were to dealing with the situation. And I could see how resourceful you were. I'm so proud of the young man my son has become."

"Aww, Mom . . ."

"Go to bed," she said. "Get some sleep. You'll need it."

Matt said good night and headed to his room. He'd done everything he could.

But Matt didn't sleep much that night. He tossed and turned in his bed, knowing full well that when the sun rose again, he might have to lead his fellow Net Force Explorers into an actual battle. As the hours before daybreak dragged on, Matt Hunter struggled in the darkness with his fears and doubts.

"The Bosnian Crisis that flared up in 2007, our first major war of the twenty-first century, began much like the First World War in the twentieth century," Dr. Lanier told them as the morning pre-flight history lesson began. "A series of alliances brokered by the United Nations and separate European nations led to a domino effect."

As Dr. Lanier spoke, a map of Europe appeared in three dimensions behind him.

"When internal squabbling heated up between the Bosnian Serbs and their Muslim neighbors, the old North Atlantic Treaty Organization nations found themselves at odds with the Russian government and its Eastern European allies," the professor continued.

The Net Force Explorers were tense and anxious as they listened to the professor's briefing. Right before the class began, Matt had spoken to them all. He'd couldn't tell them about Raptor, but he had told them that Julio's life and the lives of his parents and sister depended on their actions today.

The Net Force Explorers were determined not to fail.

"For two nations, Japan and Germany, this would be the first war, outside of some United Nation joint actions, that they actively participated in since the Second World War," Dr. Lanier lectured. "A multitude of factors, from the disastrous long-term results of the Dayton Peace Accord to the West's reluctance to offer the Russians full NATO membership, led to the short but bloody war. But we are not here to discuss the political decisions that caused the war."

Another map appeared on the wall behind the professor, this one of southeastern Europe. Red lines were superimposed over Greece. The lines turned right and led into Bosnia.

"Forces from the United States and Germany patrolled what came to be called the Sarajevo Corridor," Dr. Lanier said. "Fighters and bombers from land bases in Greece and from carriers in the Mediterranean flew daily missions into Bosnia. A second corridor, through Romania, was patrolled by the British, French, and Japanese," Lanier said as a green arrow appeared, tracing that patrol area.

"In these corridors, the Allies were opposed both by the small Serbian Air Force, flying old MiG-23 Floggers and MiG-29 Fulcrums, and by the more modern Russian Air Force, armed with the formidable Mikoyan 1-42 and MiG-33's." As the professor spoke, schematics of all the aircraft appeared behind him and rotated so that the Net Force Explorers could see the planes from every direction.

"An unwillingness among the Allies and Russia to commit large-scale ground forces to the war led to the Bosnian Crisis becoming a war of air strikes and counterstrikes among the major powers, and a war of attrition among the original combatants,'' Lanier said.

The flat-screen on the wall filled with images of fighters racing through the sky, missiles launching from wing pylons to strike targets on the ground below, and general footage of American pilots scrambling for their F-15E Strike Eagles, F-16 Fighting Falcons, F-22 Lightning II's, and F-117 Stealth Fighters.

''This air war soon became a machine-versus-machine showdown, altogether unlike the contests you've previously participated in. Most of the Allied planes lost in combat were taken out by ground-based surface-to-air missiles, or SAMs. These SAMs were launched both from permanent installations and from mobile platforms. In order for the fighter pilots and bombers to fly their missions through the war zone, the first priority of the Allied forces was to disable the SAM sites. But they weren't easy to find.

''Some of the intelligence for tactical strikes was gathered by satellite, augmented by real-time surveillance video from unmanned drone planes,'' Lanier said.

All around them, holograms of the small radio-controlled aircraft filled the air.

''In addition to being useful for collecting information, the drones also served as launch platforms for a variety of small munitions, and pinpointed targets for guided missiles.''

Camouflaged missile launchers ringed by antiaircraft guns appeared before them, framed by the little drones. An AGM-130 precision-guided modular glide bomb hurtled through the air above the target, seemingly coming from nowhere, as the Net Force Explorers watched. The missile landed and the SAM emplacement exploded.

''The use of these flying drones increased the Allies' available airpower by freeing planes and pilots from high-risk missions. The drones were cheap and easy to produce, while the expensive equipment to control and monitor them stayed safely behind the lines, so large quantities could be deployed and large losses of the drones sustained.

''But some of the intelligence still had to be gathered the hard way. This was often true of SAM sites. Drones weren't often attractive enough targets to bring SAMs into play. The best way to find the launchers was to home in on the radar or IR beacon that they used to guide their missiles to the targets, then shoot a HARM anti-radiation or IRST infrared search-and-track missile at it. But they only turned on those beacons when worthwhile targets were within range. Pilots flying F-15's outfitted as Wild Weasels, or SAM assault aircraft, made this their specialty. They would fly escort for strike aircraft, and when the SAM batteries prepared to launch their deadly weapons into the sky, the Wild Weasels would destroy them by firing missiles at close range, dodging the SAMs, often flying in the teeth of covering fire. It was one of the most dangerous missions of the war. Once the SAMs were taken out, then the bombers and fighters could proceed to their targets. This kind of flying was originally done by F-100's and F-105's in the late 1960's in Vietnam, and later by F-4Gs in 1991 during the Gulf War.

"In addition to the support of Wild Weasels, fighter aircraft depended on many other aircraft to successfully accomplish their missions. In-flight refueling by tanker planes extended the range and hours of operation of all the aircraft in the theater of operations. And airborne warning and control planes, or AWACs, like the E-3 Sentry provided long-range target acquisition and identification, as well as control, coordination, and communication between the Allied forces. Because of the Sentries, every Allied pilot knew where every other plane in the sky was, and which aircraft were friendly and which were not.

"From the start, the Western allies had the edge in technology, but were unwilling either to commit sufficient ground troops to control the battlefield or to inflict from the air the kind of civilian casualties and collateral damage necessary to end the war completely. That kept things fairly evenly matched. Until near the end . . ."

His voice trailed off as a blurry hologram of one of the most remarkable military weapons ever built flashed into three dimensional form before their eyes.

"In the last months of the war, the Russians introduced their technological marvel, the MiG-44. Faster and much more maneuverable than anything the Allies could field, armed with a

30mm GSh-301 cannon and sixteen hardpoints, capable of carrying up to ten thousand kilograms of guided bombs, missiles, and rockets, it was a far better platform than anything the Allies were flying.''

Every one of the Net Force Explorers suddenly got anxious. None of them wanted to go up against that aircraft. Dr. Lanier turned himself to admire the incredible machine.

"Hand-built by a team of technicians at the A. I. Mikoyan Aviation Scientific-Industrial Complex, led by the brilliant aircraft designer Igor Nikolayev, the MiG-44 could have changed the tide of the war if it had come soon enough, and in large enough numbers."

Dr. Lanier turned back to the class.

"Fortunately, it did not. Only eleven were built. Flown remotely by pilots connected to the control panel with full virtual technology, the 44's were freed from the physical constraints placed on most aircraft by the presence of fragile humans on board. They could dive and turn more sharply, and execute higher-speed maneuvers—maneuvers that were within the physical capabilities of most contemporary jets, but that generated G-forces that would kill an on-board pilot. They could perform up to the full potential of the machinery, not merely up to the limits imposed by the presence of the pilots."

Dr. Lanier's voice rose to dramatically punctuate his next sentence. "Those eleven MiGs accounted for almost twenty-five percent of the air-to-air casualties of the Bosnian Crisis," he said.

Dr. Lanier smiled, a gesture that was meant to reassure them.

"Of course," he continued, "in the interest of fairness, the Russian team you will be facing won't be equipped with MiG-44's."

Yeah, Matt thought ominously. *And there weren't supposed to be Messerschmitt 262's either!*

"Aerial combat in 2007 was very different from the missions you've flown previously in this competition, for several reasons. The kind of close-contact dogfighting that was the hallmark of previous wars was no longer practical in the Bosnian conflict. The weapons were computer-controlled, and long-range. In most cases they were aimed and launched without the pilot ever making visual contact with the target,'' Lanier said. ''The Wild Weasel missions were notable exceptions to that, however. You'll get to find out in person.

''In this simulation some of you will be flying F-15's outfitted for Wild Weasel missions. The rest of you will fly the F-22's they're protecting.

''I'll see you later, in the battle simulators.''

The Net Force Explorers gathered around the roster on the illuminated board.

''You'll be happy to note that Dieter is on *our* side this time,'' David Gray said.

Relieved, is more like it, Matt thought.

Matt scanned the names of the Russians. ''Oh, no,'' he gasped.

''What?'' Mark asked.

''The guy who came in third last year, Sergei Shonin, the Russian hotshot—he's on the other side.''

''Don't worry,'' Andy Moore said grandly, jabbing his thumb into his chest. ''*I'll* take care of *him*.''

Matt, David, Mark, and Megan all exchanged glances.

''I'm so happy that the *old* Andy has returned,'' Megan said with dripping sarcasm.

Everyone burst into laughter, including Andy. Then, their tensions released, the team headed off to the simulators.

15

In Corteguay, as dawn was breaking, the SEALs crouched in tall grasses, watching a curving stretch of rutted dirt road that led to a small wooden bridge over a deep gorge. With their cammo-painted faces behind the visors of their patterned smartsuits, the soldiers were virtually invisible in the jungle.

Stegar checked his digital watch. The truck from Adello was late. Of course, it had been late almost as often as it had been on time in the last few weeks, so the colonel wasn't worried.

Yet.

Then he heard a sharp whistle. It sounded almost exactly like the call of a local jungle bird, but Stegar knew the difference. The whistle came from Lieutenant Knappert, high in the trees above, warning them that a vehicle was coming. But not the one they were waiting for.

As they peered through the vegetation, the lights of a vehicle approached. A battered Hummer bumped down the road. The ancient military vehicle carried only a driver. It sped past their position and continued across the rickety wooden bridge.

Stegar remembered that Hummer from the intel photos. The driver of that vehicle—whoever he was—was a frequent visitor to the compound, coming and going once or twice a week. But according to the latest satellite photos, the Hummer had been there yesterday, too. Two visits in two days was unusual.

The colonel wondered if anything was amiss in the political prison.

Five minutes later, a second, subtly different whistle echoed down to their positions. Stegar turned around.

"Go!" he whispered to two SEALs wrapped in black blankets who were crouched beside him. He could hear leaves rustling behind him as Knappert climbed down from her observation post.

The men unwrapped themselves from their blankets and hurried out onto the dirt road, dragging behind them a large fallen tree limb they'd scavenged from the jungle. They left it in the road, completely blocking the way, then hid in the surrounding jungle vegetation.

When the truck came around the bend, the driver saw the obstruction on the roadway and slammed on the brakes. They could hear the squeals of the tires as the vehicle skidded, and the angry cries of the young driver too. Those who spoke Spanish could understand him as he cursed fluently, then instructed the men in the back to get out and "move the bleeping branch away from this stinking excuse for a road." As the truck shrieked to a halt, Knappert slipped out from behind a tree and ran toward the driver's side of the cab. The rest of the SEALs went on alert in their hiding places, their guns ready.

Matt flew his F-15G Wild Weasel in the point position of the flight pattern, with Mark Gridley on his wing. Behind and above them flew David, Megan, and Andy Moore in F-22's.

Matt and Mark's job was to scout out the enemy, draw Bosnian ground fire to see where the surface-to-air missile launchers were located, and destroy them so that their fellow Net Force Explorers could fly safely on to make tactical bombing strikes. Along the way, they could perhaps even hit a few more targets of their own.

Wild Weasels were generally older jets that flew in a nice straight line to draw enemy fire for what the enemy thought would be an easy kill. Once Matt and Mark had a fix on the enemy's SAM launch sites, they were responsible for taking them out. Matt wasn't sure where the military came up with the name "Weasel" for this job.

He'd have figured "Sitting Duck" would be more appropriate.

Before they left, the Net Force Explorers were briefed on what to expect, and what to engage in virtual combat. Anything on the ground was fair game, but they had to be careful not to engage friendly fighters in the skies. Dieter and the Germans would be flying patrol out here. And so would Sergei and his Russians. The Russians were fair game.

"Ground fire! Ground fire!" Mark said. Matt's own computer console started screaming, indicating the presence of enemy radar targeted on his plane. Just ahead of them, Matt saw surface-to-air missiles launch. Matt took a deep breath, then dipped and jinked his fighter, dodging the SAMS while he shot a HARM anti-radar air-to-surface missile at the offending ground installation. Behind him, Mark did the same. The missiles followed the targeting radars right to their sources.

A satisfying explosion, followed by a few secondaries, indicated that one Bosnian SAM site was gone. But, of course, there were many, many more.

Some of which began shooting at them now.

The air was filled with surface-to-air missiles. Matt jinked his plane again, narrowly avoiding a hit on his wing. Mark Gridley had to eject chaff—strips of Mylar coated with aluminum—into the air to fool a missile target sensor into thinking the mass of metal was an airplane.

Fortunately, the ruse worked, and the missile exploded harmlessly in the middle of the metal-flake cloud. All the while, even as they were dodging for their lives, they continued firing missiles at the SAM sites. More explosions on the ground reflected their success.

As quickly as it began, the missile assault ended. Matt, to his surprise, realized his heart was pumping and his hands were sweaty and shaking. And this was only the beginning.

I have to calm down, he thought. *I have to concentrate on the mission.* Frantically, Matt reviewed the pre-flight briefing in his mind. What did Dr. Lanier say about the missiles?

If they stopped, it didn't necessarily mean all the SAM launchers were out of commission. Sometimes it meant trouble was coming from the skies.

"Stay alert!" Matt said. "I think the Russians are close."

"I got a bandit on my scope!" Mark Gridley said frantically.

"Incoming!" David Gray shouted. Their heads-up displays came alive with symbols as the Russian fighters closed within targeting distance of them, more than fifty miles away. . . .

Lieutenant Knappert's hands were shaking as Stegar gathered the SEALs around the truck. The fight had been short and decisive. All the Cubans, the young driver, the fat Corteguan sergeant, and the three technicians were secured—unconscious, stripped of their clothing, tied up, and about to be hidden in the jungle.

Once the truck was stopped, Knappert was responsible for taking out the driver, while the rest of the SEALs coldly selected their targets, all but one of whom were out in the middle of the road trying to move the branch.

When Stegar gave the silent signal, they fired their stun weapons. The guns made a quiet coughing sound as they spat the non-lethal taser rounds. One of the SEALs walked to the open back of the truck, dragged the startled Corteguan sergeant out of it, and knocked him out with his zipknife.

They'd chosen their weapons with care. Bullet-riddled windshields would be hard to explain to the guards at the compound. Unfortunately, the young driver had apparently seen something to make him suspicious. He ducked, and Knappert was unable to drag him out of the cab fast enough. To her surprise, the frightened private produced a pistol and shot her at point-blank range.

Knappert took the shot on the front of her smartsuit, and the energy of the round as it struck her felt like a fist to the gut, but she kept her grip on the young driver and took him down with her as she fell. Breathing hard, Knappert rolled over on top of the boy, holding her knife to his neck.

The young man simply froze there, terrified by the soldier his bullet had not killed, until another SEAL helped her up and took charge of the prisoner.

Lieutenant Knappert looked down at the youth, now lying trussed up at her feet. He couldn't have been more than fifteen, and his collar and shirt were covered with motor oil. He might have taken her out, if he'd thought to raise his weapon just a little higher and go for the weakest link in the smartsuit, the joint between the headpiece and the body of the suit.

"You okay, Lieutenant?" one of the men asked.

"No harm done," Knappert assured him. But after the SEALs had dealt with the Corteguayans, her hands were still shaking.

Lieutenant Knappert, for all her training and all her bravado, had never had anything like that happen before today. She'd never been shot at from point-blank range. She didn't like it, and she wasn't going to let it happen again. The next time, her target wouldn't see her coming. She willed her hands to steady, and sheathed her knife.

Air-to-air combat in the year 2007 was a strange thing. Matt and Mark were much too far from their enemies to see them—the sky was apparently empty of anything but Net Force Explorers and their planes. And he fervently hoped the Russians didn't know where he was yet. But that was unlikely. Matt's computer gave him the real story, beeping steadily when his flight path put him at a favorable angle to fire his missiles at the Russians, shrieking a warning when the Russians were in a position to target him. And all the while his F-15 was whistling through the sky at twice the speed of sound, maneuvering in high-G-force turns that pushed his body to the limit of his endurance.

Every time he spun his plane into a tight turn, the forces of inertia pushed Matt deeply into his seat, sometimes with as much as eight times the force of gravity. Though he wore a special flight suit to help counteract the effects of the G-forces, he still had to tense the muscles in his lower body to keep blood from pooling in his legs. He'd black out if he couldn't maintain sufficient blood circulation to supply his brain through the turn.

At the speeds he was flying, the slightest mistake could be fatal. If Matt lost consciousness, or even had a partial blackout—"a gray-out"—and his plane went out of control, he'd be just as dead as if he'd been hit by a Russian missile.

He had a small arsenal of air-to-air missiles in addition to his HARM missiles—AMRAAM AIM-120's, Sparrow AIM-7's, and Sidewinder AIM-9's—some of which could home in on the radar or infrared signature of an enemy plane, and were what were called fire-and-forget missiles. When Matt fired them, their long-burn-time solid-fuel rockets propelled them to the target at four or five times the speed of sound. Other missiles he carried had to be guided to a specific target manually by video, by satellite, or by laser beacon. With the missiles he carried, he could splash a plane more than fifty miles away.

But to get tone and fire a missile, he first had to get a Russian plane, too far away to see, lined up properly to target it, all without attracting return fire. In the aerial battles of the twenty-first century, the pilot who found his enemy first had a tremendous advantage. Matt had been successful at it so far today, but the day was young yet. Gritting his teeth, Matt yanked the stick and guided his jet into yet another tight turn.

Andy Moore, his wingman David Gray lost to SAM fire, jockeyed into position to take out another MiG. The image of the enemy plane filled his HUD—heads-up display—as he got closer. Andy followed the Russian in the display until he got tone, a steady sound that indicated that his computer targeting system was locked on the enemy.

Then he fired.

A Sidewinder air-to-air missile left its hardpoint attachment and streaked toward the MiG. He watched its flight in his display. The missile ran up the Russian's tailpipe a minute or so later.

Andy immediately began searching for other targets.

Megan, meanwhile, had her hands full. She'd targeted a two-plane formation and launched a pair of air-to-air missiles at them. After she pulled up and changed headings, she saw one MiG explode. The other jinked away, spitting chaff. Megan streaked onward, and lost the image of that one on her display. She hoped it was destroyed, but didn't have time to be sure of it.

There were other MiGs closing in on her.

Mateo noticed there were five Cubans guarding the gate today. When he looked up, he spotted another, sitting in a camouflaged nest in the trees above and behind the square concrete structure. That one had a machine gun pointed at the road leading up to the facility.

After he drove through the steel gates and parked his Hummer, Mateo had a single question for the guards.

"What is wrong?" Mateo said.

The Cuban shrugged his narrow shoulders. "We have been placed on alert," the man said.

After the retinal scan Mateo rode the elevator down to the underground chamber. When he got out he noticed that the two assassins were hooked up to American-built virtual-reality rigs, probably bought through shell companies in Guatemala and Nicaragua. The men inside were already in the chairs in a veeyar trance. The Cuban was hooked up to some kind of intravenous drip, probably providing a supply of Drex-Dream.

The master approached.

"Mateo, my friend," he said smoothly. "Your nephew is attempting another escape. He amuses me too much for me to simply kill him and put an end to it. Besides, I may yet need his cooperation or his family's before the election is over. There will be U.N. observers everywhere as the balloting approaches.

"So now my assassins are ready to find him, wherever he is on the Net, and once they've found him we'll put an end to his little mental voyages. We'll follow his path back here, and close down the door he's using to force his way out."

"Is that what all the guards are about?" Mateo asked. "Surely it is unnecessary to have men with weapons at the ready when all you have to do is take my nephew out of that rig and put him in a cage somewhere until the election is over."

"Oh, no," the man said. "Your nephew is merely a small distraction to help me pass the time. I also have intelligence that suggests that the Norteamericanos will hit the prison tonight or tomorrow."

"Fine then," Mateo said, pushing past him.

"Where are you going?" the man asked, a hint of anger in his voice.

Almost against his will, Mateo turned back. Years of conditioning took control of his actions.

"With your permission," Mateo Cortez said, "I would like to check on my niece."

Megan fell next, her jet targeted by the MiG she'd nearly taken out. She twisted and dodged to escape a heat-seeking missile locked on to her aircraft. All her countermeasures failed her and she couldn't shake the thing. Her F-22 fighter exploded, the front end of the aircraft spinning to earth in a spectacular fireball.

Matt scanned the skies for his wingman, or any of the other Net Force Explorers. As he looked, an insistent warning shriek came from his targeting computer.

Matt cursed, twisting his head from side to side and scanning his displays to find the source of the problem. A missile had locked onto his plane, but he couldn't see where it was coming from.

I'm gonna die, he thought. Then his mind recoiled—this was no time for pessimism. He twisted the stick wildly, pushing his plane to its limits to evade the attack, all the while spewing chaff into the air and blasting the area around him with electronic countermeasures, or ECMs, to fool the missile.

Something worked.

The sky on his right seemed to explode, bathing him in hot, white light. Chunks of shrapnel followed, one of them punching into his fuselage, but no red lights appeared on his control panel. He'd gotten lucky, really lucky. If he'd taken any real damage to his plane or his systems, it would have shown up on the console.

"Matt, check your six!" Mark Gridley said. Matt's HUD indicated the presence of another MiG on his tail. At that moment, his targeting computer warned Matt that the Russian was locked onto his fighter.

As Matt watched, the symbol on his HUD changed from "MISSILE LOCK" to "LAUNCH."

Matt steered his plane into a steep dive to boost his airspeed, twisting and turning to elude the weapon, with the Russian missile on him like moss on a log. . . .

• • •

Dieter Rosengarten and his Berliners spotted the air battle from a distance. They hung back for a moment, gaining altitude for their attack.

As he approached the battle, Rosengarten searched the sky for another aircraft, one painted all in orange, with black stripes. He wasn't sure it would even show up, but he was ready if it did. . . .

Andy Moore was cut off and fighting the battle of his life. Three MiG-33's were on him, and he only had two missiles left. He knew it was only a matter of time before they got him.

But he refused to give up. *At least I can lead these Russians away from Matt and Mark,* he thought.

Then his warning system told him that two missiles had been launched at him. He danced on his wing and turned into the path of the missiles, hoping that the less-maneuverable projectiles could not follow his moves.

It worked. Both missiles flashed past his wing, and a MiG entered his line of fire. Without hesitating, Andy switched to his cannon and depressed the trigger.

The MiG-33 disintegrated.

But his warning system began to shrill again as two more missiles locked on to his aircraft. Oddly, the tone died almost immediately. Then a bright flash lit up the sky behind him. Andy turned and saw three German Eurofighter EF2000's streaking toward him.

Dieter and his friends had taken out both MiGs and missiles. *"Danke Schoen,"* Andy Moore said gratefully.

"You're welcome," Dieter said as he flashed past Andy's wing and was gone. . . .

Matt rocketed downward. The munitions factory they were supposed to target was out there somewhere on the ground. Right in front of him, in fact. He waited until it was almost too late, until he was almost sure to crash into it, then pulled out of his dive as sharply as he could without snapping the wings off his plane or blacking out. The heat-seeking missile behind him continued on its course, locked now onto the smokestacks of the factory. As Matt raced back into the sky, a ferocious explosion ripped into the building, then further explosions as the weapons and fuels stockpiled within the factory blew up and magnified the effects of the original bomb.

Target destroyed—and with the enemy's own missile.

But Matt didn't have time to gloat. There was still a MiG-33 out there with his name on it—one he had to outwit or outmaneuver if he was going to warn Julio. His cockpit warning lights started flashing and his buzzers began to shriek at him. The Russian was right behind him!

When the Russian on his tail failed to fire a missile, Matt knew that the pilot must be out of them. That was good, because Matt still had two left. But if Matt couldn't shake this guy, he knew he could never gain an attack position.

As he jinked through the sky, Matt searched for a solution. The Russian opened up with his cannon, and tracers flashed past Matt's cockpit. Matt redoubled his efforts to survive.

Then he remembered Julio's stunt from the previous year. When a Russian had been on Julio's tail, Julio had put down his flaps and lifted his nose. It had almost stalled his plane, but it got the Russian off his back and into Julio's crosshairs.

Here goes, Matt said as he dropped his flaps.

The MiG streaked past Matt, and moved right into missile range. Matt's F-15 did almost stall, but he steadied her in time to fire a missile up the Russian's tailpipe.

"Got ya!" Matt said in triumph.

"Good shooting, *mi amigo*!" a familiar voice said.

Matt felt a rush of triumph.

"JULIO!" he yelled as a black and orange fighter—an F-22—appeared beside him.

"Listen closely, *Jefe*." Matt said. "I have a lot to tell you. . . ."

"There are six Cuban guards at the compound," Lieutenant Knappert said as she returned to the truck after a quick sortie around the pumping station. "And a brand-new machine gun nest in the tree above it . . ."

Stegar's blood chilled at the news. *Could they have been warned?* he wondered. But it was too late to worry about it.

"Okay," Stegar said, calling the others to him. "This is what we're going to do. . . ."

. . .

For almost two minutes, Matt and Julio were left alone. Matt told his friend about the raid—the predicted plan, the number of personnel taking part, and when it was going down. Julio and Matt both realized that time was running out.

"I must get back," Julio said.

"What are you going to do?" Matt asked.

"Kill the security system," Julio said. "And shut down the veeyar too. That way, our jailers can't harm my family."

"But what about you?" Matt asked. "When you take the system down, you'll still be in an active rig. You can go into neural shock if you don't go through proper procedures before exiting veeyar—you know that. If you're still hooked up to the system when you crash it . . ."

Julio did not reply. He merely smiled at his friend. "A soldier does not think of such things," Julio whispered. Then he sighed. "You have been a good friend," he said, his voice filled with a sadness that was audible over the radio. "I must go now, before they come to get me. . . ."

Suddenly, another voice crackled in Matt's ears. "I think the enemy is already here," Dieter Rosengarten said. "Check your six."

Matt looked at his display. To his horror, two MiGs that could only be 44's were streaking across the sky. No other type of plane could possibly achieve the speed of these bogeys. Given their trajectory, their target had to be Julio's orange fighter plane.

"Mayday! Mayday!" Matt said. "Net Force Explorers! I need you! Julio, get out of here!"

Dieter and another German flew between Julio and the attackers. Matt joined them, forming a line of defense between Julio and the MiG-44s.

"We don't have a chance, you know," Dieter said calmly.

"Wanna bet?" Matt said as he hit the afterburners and rushed toward the enemy fighters.

Matt fired his two missiles the moment he had a missile lock.

They didn't even make the jets change course.

The first MiG, painted black with a Cuba Libre symbol on its wing, easily destroyed both missiles. The defense system in the high-tech Russian aircraft sent intense electronic countermeasures through the sky, exploding the projectiles long before they were within range of his plane.

Matt kept coming. If he could, he planned to ram one of them, to do anything to protect Julio until he was safely away from the simulation.

As Matt pointed the nose of his F-15 at the black MiG, the jet shot around him, faster and more maneuverable than Matt's plane would ever be. Matt flashed past his target, cursing.

The second MiG, with a Rising Sun logo on its wing, launched a missile at the oncoming Germans. Before the missile reached them, its nose cone burst apart as several small projectiles blasted away from it, enveloping one of the Euro-fighters. Dieter's wingman blew up in a spectacular explosion. The shock waves rocked Dieter's fighter, which probably saved him, as several tiny missiles streaked through the space his jet had occupied a split second before.

"Matt, they're using Swarm missiles!" Dieter yelled.

As Dieter regained control of his fighter, and Matt turned to attack the enemy, the MiG-44's closed in on Julio's orange airplane.

"They've got a lock on me," Julio said. "I don't know what I can do to shake them!"

"Just call 'Rescues-R-Us,'" Andy Moore said, right before his fighter slammed into the Cuban MiG in a repeat performance of his suicidal move of the other day.

Mark Gridley appeared at that same moment. His F-22 cut between Julio's plane and the remaining MiG-44. The multiple-target individual warheads burst from the Swarm missile and tore his fighter jet apart, but he stopped them from hitting Julio.

"Your friends are very brave," Dieter remarked as he hit his afterburners and streaked toward the remaining MiG-44. The Japanese assassin easily avoided the German, and as Dieter raced past, he spat missiles at him.

Dieter's plane exploded—marring the German student's otherwise excellent record.

But while the MiG pilot concentrated on killing the German, he'd forgotten about Matt. The Net Force Explorer came around the MiG and streaked toward its tail.

"Good luck, Julio!" Matt said as his plane slammed into the MiG-44. . . .

The battered truck rumbled down the road toward the compound.

The Cuban guard at the gate looked at his friend. "It's about time," he said. He got up and walked in front of the truck to begin the ID checks. But to his surprise, the vehicle did not even slow down. It just kept coming.

Too late, the Cuban snatched his pistol and pointed it at the driver. But the man behind the wheel hit the gas pedal. As the Cuban leaped out of the way, the truck slammed through the gate.

In the tree, the machine gunner turned around, cocked his gun, and pointed it at the truck. At that moment he felt the platform vibrate under his feet. Before he could make a move Lieutenant Knappert took him out. She grabbed his gun and used it to eliminate the remaining Cuban guards.

The SEALs emerged from the truck and rushed toward the pumping station building. Colonel Stegar pulled out a wad of plastic explosives, ready to place the charge on the steel door of the bunker. But to his surprise, the interior lock clicked and the door opened.

A Cuban guard on the inside of the bunker was just as surprised. Stegar dropped him before he could react.

The colonel rolled into the building, and took out a second man, a technician.

But as fast as Stegar was, he wasn't fast enough. As the man in the lab coat fell, he hit the alarm.

In the underground facility, the master stood over the still-twitching bodies of his virtual assassins.

"They knew the price of failure," he said to Mateo, and holstered his weapon. As the echo of the shots he'd just fired died away, the security screens went blank.

He blinked. "Something is wrong!" he said. The chamber was soundproofed, so they could hear nothing from above. The man picked up the security phone, planning to call the guards above.

No dial tone.

"It's the Norteamericanos!" he said. "They are here!"

As if to punctuate his statement, the alarm klaxon began to blare.

"We are under attack!" the Corteguayan said. He turned, wild-eyed, to the computer monitor. Even as he watched, the system shut down completely. He slammed his fist down on the control button that would send thousands of volts of electricity through the hostages' bodies, killing them instantly, but nothing happened.

He whirled, his eyes moving from side to side like a trapped animal's. Just then, he and Mateo heard the elevator cage begin to descend—the retinal-scan security system had probably been shut down too.

"The Yanquis come!" he said. "But they will not get their prize!"

With that, he raced across the room, pushing past Mateo, to the bodies strapped to the tables. He placed the barrel of his pistol against Ramon Cortez's head.

Ramon groaned and stirred, waking from his veeyar-induced trance.

"NO!" Mateo shouted, rushing the man responsible for what he'd become. But Mateo had too far to go. Coldly, his master raised the pistol and fired at his rebellious creature. Mateo clutched his chest, and his master fired again. And again.

Then, turning from Mateo, the man pointed the muzzle of his gun at Ramon Cortez a second time.

Mateo's desperate move had bought Ramon just enough time. Before the man could shoot, the elevator doors opened wide, and Colonel Stegar opened fire. The Corteguayan fell to the ground, dead before he could pull his own trigger.

The last technician threw up his hands in surrender, and Lieutenant Knappert grabbed him by the collar and threw him to the floor.

"Who's that?" she asked, keeping her eyes on her prisoner while motioning her head toward the man Colonel Stegar had killed.

"Believe it or not, he was supposed to be on our side," the colonel said. "His name was Manuel Arias."

Epilogue

A month later, Matt sat on the roof observation deck at Net
Force Explorers' virtual headquarters. He was alone, and he'd
been contemplating the sky above. He'd imagined for a moment that he, Mark Gridley, and Julio Cortez were flying up
there in a Sopwith Camel, a P-51 Mustang, or an F-15 fighter.

But he knew that it could never be.

Matt had had to wait until he got home the night of the
Bosnian simulation to learn what had happened. Not surprisingly, given his experiences with the State Department over
the last few days, Matt's source of information wasn't the
government. He found out from the HoloVid International
News. It was the lead story.

According to the news anchor, a team of Navy SEALs had
gone into Corteguay and rescued presidential candidate Ramon
Cortez and his family from a political prison. Walter Paulson
was at the press conference as the State Department spokes-
man. He told the world how a brave team of Americans had
made Corteguay safe for democracy.

It was an almost perfect mission, he said proudly.

Almost.

But Julio was dead. He'd released his family from inside
the computer program, but he'd never made it back himself.
By the time the soldiers got to him, neural shock had taken
hold, and in a place so isolated from proper medical facilities

they'd been unable to save him. Matt felt a terrible sense of loss. An ache in his heart he'd never felt before.

Now I know how Andy Moore feels every day, he thought sadly. *How does he cope with the loss of his father?*

Matt heard the door open behind him, but he didn't turn around. Megan O'Malley moved beside him. She stood for a while in silence, and watched the sky with him.

"Have you ever heard of the Flying Dutchman?" she asked suddenly.

"Nope," Matt said, shaking his head.

"It's a crazy legend about a ghost ship with a ghost captain who sails the Seven Seas forever," she said. "There's a holo of it."

"Uh-huh," Matt grunted.

"I always thought that if the captain loved the sea, as most sea captains must, then sailing them forever wasn't such a bad thing," she concluded.

They stood in silence for another minute.

"The results of the Century of Military Aviation competition were just announced," Megan said.

Matt looked at her. Because the Net Force Explorers had done so poorly, they'd not gone on to the next round, or any of the later ones with experimental aircraft. Matt had completely forgotten about it.

"Dieter Rosengarten won the Ace of Aces trophy," she continued.

Matt smiled. "I'm happy for him," he said.

"Well," Megan smiled. "He just showed up in the Lounge."

"Dieter?" Matt said, surprised.

"Yup," she said. "Said he almost lost the final round, but a friend of ours appeared and got him out of a jam."

Matt turned and met Megan's gaze. "You mean?"

"He said an orange plane with black tiger stripes appeared out of nowhere and nailed Sergei," she said.

Matt got choked up. "Do you think it's possible?" he asked.

"Sure," Megan said with a smile. "He got out of that prison, didn't he? I think he left his mark on that simulator when he forced his way into it so many times to try to contact us. I think that the character he created for himself in that simulator is still intact.''

Matt nodded, his heart filled with happiness for the first time in days.

"It's kind of fitting," Megan continued. "What better place for Julio to leave behind a piece of himself than in a flight simulator?''

Matt continued to stare at the sky for another minute or so.

"I can't wait," he said abruptly. Megan blinked, puzzled. Matt turned and faced her.

"I can't wait until next year's competition," he explained. "We'll have an edge—a secret weapon named Julio Cortez.''